WITHDRAWN
No longer the property of the
Boston Public Library.
Sale of this material benefited the Library

the **americas**

ADVISORY BOARD
Irene Vilar, series editor

Edna Acosta-Belén
Daniel Alarcón
Frederick Luis Aldama
Esther Allen
Homero Aridjis
Harold Augenbraum
Stanley H. Barkan
Junot Díaz
Dedi Felman
Rosario Ferré
Jean Franco
Rigoberto González
Edith Grossman
Naomi Lindstrom
Adriana V. López

Jaime Manrique
Mirta Ojito
Gavin O'Toole
Bud Parr
Margaret Sayers Peden
Gregory Rabassa
Luis J. Rodriguez
Lissette Rolón-Collazo
Rossana Rosado
Daniel Shapiro
Mónica de la Torre
Silvio Torres-Saillant
Doug Unger
Oscar Villalon

Timote

A Novel

José Pablo Feinmann

Translated by David William Foster

Introduction by Douglas Unger

Texas Tech University Press

Originally published by Planeta as *Timote,* copyright © 2009 by José Pablo Feinmann, by arrangement with Literarische Agentu Mertin Inh. Nicole Witt e. K.,
Frankfurt am Main, Germany.

Translation copyright © 2012 by David William Foster

Work published within the framework of "SUR" Translation Support Program of
the Ministry of Foreign Affairs, International Trade and Worship of the Argentine
Republic.
   The publisher and author appreciate the financial support for translation of
Timote.

All rights reserved. No portion of this book may be reproduced in any form or by
any means, including electronic storage and retrieval systems, except by explicit
prior written permission of the publisher. Brief passages excerpted for review and
critical purposes are excepted.

This book is typeset in Fairfield. The paper used in this book meets the mini-
mum requirements of ANSI/NISO Z39.48–1992 (R1997). ∞

Designed by Kasey McBeath
Cover illustration by Irma Sizer

Library of Congress Cataloging-in-Publication Data
Feinmann, José Pablo.
   [Timote. English]
   Timote : a novel / José Pablo Feinmann ; translated by David William Foster ;
introduction by Douglas Unger.
         p. cm. — (The Americas)
   Originally published by Planeta as Timote, 2009 by José Pablo Feinmann.
   Summary: "A fictionalization of the 1970 abduction and execution of Argen-
tinean general and former president Pedro Eugenio Aramburu"— Provided by
publisher.
   ISBN 978-0-89672-806-6 (pbk. : alk. paper) — ISBN 978-0-89672-807-3
(e-book) 1. Aramburu, Pedro Eugenio, 1903-1970—Assassination—Fiction.
2. Organización Montoneros (Argentina)—Fiction. I. Foster, David William. II.
Title.
   PQ7798.16.E37T5613 2012
   863'.64—dc23   2012033483

Printed in the United States of America
12 13 14 15 16 17 18 19 20 / 9 8 7 6 5 4 3 2 1

Texas Tech University Press
Box 41037 | Lubbock, Texas 79409–1037 USA
800.832.4042 | ttup@ttu.edu | www.ttupress.org

We will build a stairway
With Aramburu's bones
So that our Evita Montonera
Can descend from Heaven

Chant of the Peronista left

Introduction

Argentine social and political realities can seem to non-Argentine readers like a complex labyrinth filled with a perplexing noise of contention and complaint, and with each new turn the threat of violence. Shock at pain and blood is followed by grief at human loss, as is appropriate in response to tragedy. An equally valid response is that of the alienated spectator in a theater of the absurd, moved by players on the sociopolitical stage to a grim, involuntary cynicism combined with a sickening flip of the stomach: a physical reaction to irony—or, as philosopher Henri Bergson put it, the recognition that *this much, at least, is . . .*

José Pablo Feinmann's postmodern historical novel *Timote* intends to evoke both responses at once. Feinmann invites tragedy and absurdist irony as valid readings of dramatized events he draws from the complex, almost incomprehensible tumult of Argentine history. He seems not to intend such responses to be limited to the story of *Timote*—a tense, speculative narrative of the 1970 kidnapping and execution by urban guerrillas of former dictator General Pedro Eugenio Aramburu, who led the coup that ousted legendary strongman Juan Domingo Perón from elected, democratic power fourteen years before. On the contrary: the assassination of Aramburu is presented as a source, a first shot in the war of leftist Peronist revolution and counterrevolution that would six years later—as the kidnapped general warns—lead to the unleashing of the full fury of the Argentine army during the dictatorship of the *Proceso*. This was the infamous Dirty War of 1976–83, during which the military "disappeared" as many as thirty thousand persons and committed crimes, according to Feinmann, "so atrocious that they transcend the barriers of anything dreamed possible of men in the realm of horror."

Timote presents a novelistic interpretation of sources and analyzes the historical conditions that produced the self-deluded characters of this drama of violence and revenge. As such, it might stand as a part of an explanation why such horrors happened. The novel serves also as a cautionary tale of how naïve young idealists anywhere, in any age, can talk themselves into turning away from the pursuit of justice to commit violent crimes. Feinmann's form of speculative fiction seems right, and more appropriate than the still hotly contested versions of factual events—"the fight between what is just and what is just" as one character puts it—that would mean yet one more retelling limited by the constraints and polemics of journalism. As Feinmann takes license to teach us, "Fiction does not judge. It is the most impeccable instrument created by man for the expression of the complexity of existence."

In contemporary Argentina, José Pablo Feinmann now occupies a singular position as its most important public intellectual. His prolific production encompasses more than thirty-five books: novels, essays, philosophy, plays, screenplays, and edited collections selected from his weekly cultural-political columns in *Página 12*—the preferred newspaper of the Kirchner-Fernández government that has steered Argentina, not without fierce opposition,

since the economic crisis and banking default of 2002–03 drove
the country to near dissolution as a viable society. Feinmann has
become a talk show host in recent years, bringing his guests into
Argentine living rooms to discourse broadly on culture, the arts,
politics, and ideas. His energetic and at times tangential mono-
logues rise up spontaneously from these hosted conversations
with originality, wit, and pure brilliance. They are oral treatises
in themselves—compact lectures that teach and stir up national
controversies.

Argentina and its sociopolitical conditions have obsessed
Feinmann's creative, philosophical, and historical writing for
more than four decades, as have works by the group of intellectuals in which he came of age: David Viñas, Horacio González,
Ernesto Laclau, Manuela Fingueret, and others—writers of
resistance to brutal repression. The generic range of Feinmann's
work is astonishing. In his early fiction, such as *Últimos días de la
víctima* and *Ni el tiro del final*—both made into successful movies—he achieves hardboiled crime novels with psychoanalytic
twists, books that move through dark atmospheres of violence.
During the same years, Feinmann completed *Estudios sobre el
peronismo,* a complex treatise that dissects the delirious transfor-
mation of Peronism's populist, neofascist ideology of the 1950s
into a pseudo-Marxist fantasy. Perhaps inevitably within the
context of the ongoing Cuban revolution—tied in the minds of
Argentine militants to the romantic-heroic figure of Che Guevara
(later treated by Feinmann in a stage play, *Cuestiones con Ernesto
Che Guevara*)—this delusion culminates in labor union and
student guerrilla warfare in the 1970s, against which the military
responds with criminal force.

In a previous, highly acclaimed novel, *La astucia de la razón,* Feinmann casts violence into a metaphor of terror and paranoia during the darkest period of the Dirty War. He probes the psychology of a philosopher-professor, Pablo Epstein, who suffers from testicular cancer as well as the certainty that, soon, he will be picked up and eliminated by goon squads for the simple crime of being a leftist intellectual. His neurosis is strong evidence that the most damaging effect of state terrorism is the psychopathology it causes in citizens. As does *Timote,* the novel spirals with a nonlinear structure into the past, to 1965, when Epstein falls into the seductive embrace of his first political ideas following a baroque, story-rich discussion with three fellow students about the purpose of philosophy. As in Feinmann's later philosophical-historical study *La sangre derramada*—a work that analyzes multiple ideologies that justify violence, including the horrors of the Holocaust set alongside the bloody massacres of two centuries of state terrorism in Latin America—the philosopher biopsies and examines political violence with the scientific objectivity of a pathologist switching lenses (the theories of Kant, Marx, and Sartre) on a microscope. His surgical instruments are drawn from Hegelian dialectic. Epstein and his comrades come to the activist conclusion that philosophy should be transformative. As in Sartre's *Critique of Dialectical Reason,* Hegel's concept of culture and history as a work of "Spirit" must be turned inside out by "detotalization" so that history becomes a work of *the people*— perhaps even the work of a few exceptional individuals.

Among the first bloody events that arose from this naïve revolutionary fervor was the kidnapping and execution of General Aramburu by the Montoneros, narrated in *Timote.* The novel redefines generic boundaries as it combines journalism, history, fiction, and philosophy. Its characters play out a global conclusion of Feinmann's previous philosophical study: marginalized factions that are excluded from a nation's political discourse, especially young people put down and silenced by authoritarian regimes, almost inevitably turn to violence.

Even in this reedited and condensed English translation by David William Foster presented by the Americas series, in which some baroque tangents of narrative are reshaped to serve the economy of a tenser, more straightforward plot, reading *Timote* still might seem to non-Argentines a bit like being dropped into the middle of a heated talk show discussion in Buenos Aires in which Feinmann is holding forth and insisting on his version of events. He assumes his listeners know certain facts of Argentine history: that in 1956, General Aramburu led the military coup that toppled the increasingly authoritarian government of Juan Domingo Perón and sent him into exile. A group of officers loyal to Perón, led by General Juan José Valle, organized resistance. General Aramburu arrested General Valle and ordered his execution by firing squad. Aramburu also exhumed Evita Perón's remains, fearing her popular adoration and status of secular saint would make her tomb a rallying point for opposition, so he secretly buried her body in a cemetery in Rome. Juan Perón, from his exile in Spain, called for armed struggle against the dictatorship, an "integral war" of guerrilla actions meant to destabilize the military regime. To satisfy increasingly leftist union cadres and student movements, Perón promised a social revolution in addition to a political one so as to ensure his return to power.

Leaders in the trade unions, students, and worker organizations began to build a militancy underground. By compromise between non-Peronist labor groups and the military, democracy was restored, with two presidents elected, serving from 1958 to 1966, but with severely limited capacities to govern: Arturo Frondizi and Arturo Illia. In 1966, a new army coup led by General Juan Carlos Onganía overthrew the Illia government. The Onganía dictatorship cracked down on feuding Peronist political factions, even going to the extreme of ordering the erasure of the name Perón from Argentine history books. Onganía's goon squads invaded university campuses, purging leftist faculties; they regularly harassed, rousted out, and expelled students for political activities. Resistance steadily simmered, and eventually boiled up. In the rural north, armed groups, including the Ejército Revolucionario del Pueblo (ERP), and the Movimiento Nacionalista Tacuara (MNT), modeled themselves after Cuban revolutionary ideologies but were, paradoxically, also fervently Catholic and antisemitic. A splinter faction turned away from antisemitism and briefly followed a socialist Third World cleric, Father Carlos Mugica. This strange brew of ideas combined into the contradictory socialist-religious ideologies of the group that later called itself Montoneros. The name comes from gaucho militias of the mid-nineteenth century that rode across the pampas fighting with Don Juan Manuel de Rosas, a nationalist caudillo and president who expelled an invasion then cut a deal with the British that allowed him to rule Argentina like one huge ranch for which he was the cattle baron from 1835 to 1852. In the late 1960s, Rosas and Perón became merged in populist consciousness and song—two nationalist strongmen followed by the masses. Unrest steadily grew against the Onganía regime. In June 1969, auto workers and students staged a massive strike in the city of Córdoba, put down by the military in bloody street fighting.

The stage is now set for the main characters in *Timote,* all founders of the Montoneros: the idealistic, naïve leader, Fernando Abal Medina; the communications expert and his lover—ten years his senior—Norma Arrostito; the sergeants Carlos Ramus, Blacky Sabino Navarro, Fatty Emilio Maza, and Ignacio Vélez; and the cold, Machiavellian lieutenant Mario Eduardo Firmenich, who will be one of the few to survive. Firmenich will lead the Montoneros through years of intense urban guerrilla warfare, sacrificing thousands of young lives; and improbably, Firmenich even lives to tell his own version of the same events, but perhaps *because* he survived—and just how remains a mystery—few people believe him. Feinmann assumes readers will accept his version as more credible, a foundation story of the kidnapping of Aramburu and his execution at a ranch house on the outskirts of the tiny provincial town of Timote *as it should have happened.*

In Feinmann's account, even General Aramburu expresses contempt for the Onganía dictatorship. The old general ironically comes to the same conclusion as his captors, although he expects very different, but equally fantastic, results: he believes he can force a compromise from Perón to support a truce between the feuding factions of labor, the landed oligarchy, the military, and the Yanquis in a new Peronist government that will maintain the multinational capitalist status quo. His kidnappers, however, remain leftist idealists steeped in the Montonero delusion that Perón's previous brand of authoritarian fascism can be transformed, essentially, by people power into a utopian project for egalitarian socialism. They intend to cause enough civil unrest to force Perón's return, then use him to pull off a revolution— as if the ancient demagogue would ever agree to go along with anything but the aggrandizement of his personal cult, including furthering the religious adoration of Evita as his opiate for the masses. After all, would a *military* man—a general who modeled his leadership style on Mussolini—agree to anything but his selfish accumulation of power? As General Aramburu asserts in *Timote:* "Perón's only interested in power. He'll do anything to get it." Later, he warns his naïve kidnappers, "If you bring him back, he'll fuck you."

They did, and Perón did—as Argentine readers know. Perón's return, followed by his unexpected death, set in motion the grim machineries of military takeover, terror, and violence of such horrific proportions that, two generations later, Argentina is still coming to terms with, and its most important public intellectual is still at work to discover why they came to pass. In *Timote,* José Pablo Feinmann presents one more piece of a possible solution, with complexities of existence only the very best fiction can express.

Douglas Unger

Timote

The guy who's sitting at the table. The one next to the window, which allows him to look outside, checking on things. That guy is Fernando Abal Medina, the Montonero who killed Aramburu. He killed him thirty or thirty-five days ago. Now they are going to kill him. Our story is not about his death, but about Aramburu's. The story in which Fernando kills Aramburu, far away, in Timote, an insignificant town in the vast Province of Buenos Aires, near Carlos Tejedor. If we begin here, on the night he is killed, it is to give weight, a tragic quality, to something he will say at the end of the story, when he leaves Timote with his companions. He leaves in the middle of the night in his Gladiator pickup, driving along a muddy road full of potholes like a madman, with the impunity that comes from feeling like a god—the main character in a violent but righteous event that will split the history of the country in two, a slash that runs deep, executed by his vengeful hand. Was it vengeance? Of course it was. Could it have been anything else but the punishment of a man for the atrocities he committed, for his insults against General Perón, our companion Evita, and the Peronista nation? What step comes after revenge? Firmenich, seated next to him, clenched his teeth so hard you could hear them grind, looking furious, but what could he do to get that man who was possessed out from behind the wheel? If he continues to drive like that, he's going to kill us all. And to top it all off, the Gladiator's lights aren't very good. You can't make out the road, no way. It's impossible.

"Calm down, Fernando."

What step comes after revenge? No, I'm not going to think about that now. The step after revenge is to enjoy it. That's it, that's the answer. Anything else comes later. Gaby is waiting for me now. I'll get there and tell her everything turned out fine. And then we'll fuck like winners, the best fuck of all. Gaby is so pretty. Such a good companion, a real woman.

"Did you hear me, Fernando? Calm down, I said," Pepe insists.

No response. He's talking to himself. He talks nonstop, talks and talks. But, wait. There's a magical, involuntary moment. He surprises himself, but a sentence punches its way out of his mouth. After he utters it, Fernando steps harder on the gas. The Gladiator is a gasp cutting the night, mutilating it.

The pizzeria is like all the others. Just like all the ones out here in the boondocks. It's called La Rueda, the Wheel. They didn't go out of their way to name the place. It's more like a grill than a pizzeria. Cars have wheels and cars cross fields, among the cows and the sheep. And they usually end up in one of the infinite number of grills in a country dedicated to meat, steaks, and barbecue. This country is even shaped like a steak. Borges, when Pinochet decorated him, said that Chile had the shape of a sword. It may not be heroic or glorious to have this beefy shape when just on the other side of the Andes there's a country shaped like a sword. How did we get to be like this? It's thanks to the pizzeria. Thanks to the name they gave it: La Rueda. What is

Fernando Abal Medina doing at that table? Because whatever its name, today, that pizzeria becomes a part of History. The world is about to explode. Bullets every which way, even an exploding grenade. It's about to happen. In just a little bit, but not right now. Let us suppose we turn our attention to the guy behind the counter. It would be unusual for him to like anyone. These are things you just feel in your gut. No way he's a good guy. He has the face of an insect or a pig. A pig isn't an insect, but this guy manages to look like both at the same time. Let us ask ourselves this: What's wrong with Fernando? Didn't he see him? If he had, he'd know that this guy could only be an enemy, a police snitch. Let's suppose that Fernando saw him. If he did, he didn't see him that way. The guy at the counter is a fat man just like so many others. A fat slob in a cheap pizzeria. As inoffensive as he could be. Fernando is not worried about him. He saw him, but didn't think he was dangerous. No problem. Everything's going fine.

Of course, there are posters with his face plastered all over Buenos Aires. With his face. With Firmenich's and Norma Arrostito's faces. You'd think Buenos Aires was the Far West. WANTED. That's what the poster said. They aren't pulling any punches. That's how you get people's attention. WANTED. These enemies of institutional order, democracy, the fatherland and good manners are being sought throughout the country. WANTED! Just like in the cowboy pictures or the Westerns. Those pieces of crap that Juan Villemot liked so much when they had the Film Club at the Buenos Aires National Prep School, where they showed Bergman's films. Those days were gone. To hell with art. The time has come for guns. WANTED! Him, Firmenich, and Skinny Arrostito. Which one was she? Calamity Jane. The poster has been up quite a while. Let us suppose that Fernando has seen it from a Peugeot in which he was traveling with two other companions. Let's suppose he sees the poster. There are two or three guys and a woman staring out at him. He sees the faces of the ones who killed Aramburu. They do not talk among themselves. They stare out in silence. No one attempts to share a comment with the others. Who knows what the person next to you is thinking? Like saying, "His time was up. He had it coming. It's his own fault." The other person might get furious, "What are you saying, you shithead? How can you justify killing someone like a dog?" A Peronista in her whole soul, the woman defends the first speaker, "You know why? Because he was a dog. Aramburu was a dog and they killed him like a dog. Get it?" The third person walks off. But none of this happens. At the very most the woman might say, "This country's a mess. Nothing will save it." Fernando has ordered him to stop the Peugeot he's driving. He gets out and joins the people looking at the poster. *No way does that look like me. It's a mug shot. I look like a gangster. It's enough to scare children. The photo is all fuzzy, give me a break. They're a bunch of cheapskates. Not even Gaby would recognize me.* He quickly looks at the woman and asks, "You think they're the ones? What's your opinion?"

"I can't say," she says.

"There's no saving this country," Fernando says. "My old man's been saying that since I was a little kid."

The Peugeot pulls away and Carlos Ramus, the one who's driving, tells him he's crazy, that he's being rash and they could all end up paying for his audacity. Fernando says no, that it was a chance he had to take. He'd made himself a promise. Had to show himself that poster was crap, worthless.

"Not even my mom could make me out."

But that crappy poster was going to give him away. Does he happen to look again at the fat man behind the counter? No, he doesn't. Does anyone know what Fernando Abal Medina is doing in that pizzeria, at that moment, risking his hide? What's more, sitting right in front of him at his table is Blacky Sabino Navarro. He's just sat down. A fighter in his own class. He didn't go to Tacuara, or to the Buenos Aires National College. Blacky Sabino is from Corrientes, in the north. His father was illiterate and he didn't have a pot to piss in. He came to Buenos Aires when he was twelve years old. He had to find work. He couldn't go on living the same way. In a prefabricated house. When it rains, it rains outside and it rains inside. He goes to work in a metal shop in the Colegiales neighborhood. Blacky Sabino Navarro is a laborer. He's got it all: the Corrientes lilt to his Spanish, broad shoulders, dark skin. He's a metalworker, and women think he looks like Emiliano Zapata—or Marlon Brando playing Emiliano Zapata. He doesn't miss a trick. He cheats like mad on his wife. That's how Blacky is, a slave to his hormones and unable to resist the siege of women. Tonight, in the pizzeria La Rueda, he's safe. And he takes over the leadership of the Montoneros. But on some other night he parks the red Peugeot on some forgotten street and begins to put the moves on a twenty-five-year-old chick, Mirta Silvia Silecki, who wasn't a Montonero or a Peronista or a Trotskyist—none of those things. She drives Blacky wild, but not her politics. She drives him crazy. See, not everything was politics, militancy, guns. They fuck, too. Two policemen come along. "Your ID, please." Blacky tells them they're in the trunk. The cops believe him. Blacky opens the trunk. He has a briefcase in there, with a .38 Special inside the briefcase. He takes it out in a flash and downs the two cops. Problem solved. Then, serenely, calmly, he walks over to the patrol car, opens the door and steals a submachine gun. He found it there, on the seat. But the Montoneros kick him out for amoral conduct. They go by the strict Catholic code they were taught. Theirs is the soul of monks. You may be a hothead, Blacky, and all the chicks want to get in the sack with you, but you're married, Sabino, and you owe your wife some faithfulness. We have no other choice but to cashier you. A fellow combatant who is not loyal to his companion is not going to be loyal to the organization. They kick him out and send him to Córdoba. He's not very happy there because he was born to be a leader, but he does all sorts of things. Killings, too. He tries to steal two cars in Río Cuarto, along with two companions. A bunch of cops show up. Blacky takes off into the hills. He's going to be safe there. But this time, they capture him. He's with a companion, name of Cottone. Blacky is all shot up. He's bleeding. Cottone tries to save him. Blacky tells him, "I'm in charge here and you're going to save your own skin because I say so." Cottone makes it out and they kill Blacky. That's how in July 1971 Blacky José Sabino Navarro, twenty-nine years old, dies. The leadership of the Montoneros falls to Pepe, Manolito. They call him Manolito because of Mafalda's friend in the comic strip, the Spanish immigrant kid who works in the neighborhood store, always cutting corners, a real blockhead. Chubby, too, and with bushy eyebrows that cover his eyes in a straight line. No one seems to believe in Pepe's intellectual qualities. The thing is that Blacky Sabino, who the night that Fernando Abal Medina will bleed to death all alone, saves Pepe's skin by losing him in the hills outside Córdoba. Because he told his companion, "You're going to save your own skin because I say so."

The fat man hands out the slices of pizza: focaccia, mozzarella, mozzarella with hummus, ham and red peppers. He waits and watches. He looks at Fernando out of the corner of his eye. He's afraid. What if he goes to turn him in and he kills him? Or what if he didn't kill Aramburu? Only someone who's crazy could do something like that. It must be easy to bump somebody off, child's play. Particularly someone who turned you in. The guy's dying of fright, but he's already eyeing the telephone. If he calls the police, tomorrow everyone'll be talking about him. His customers will multiply. *Look at the pizza man who had the balls to turn in Aramburu's assassin. Come to the pizzeria La Rueda. You're looking at a law-and-order Argentine. Don't waste any time, come to William Morris, a nice place in the County of Hurlingham, Province of Buenos Aires. Come and see a place anointed by posterity. Pizzeria La Rueda. Don't let them give you that line about the pizza there being crap! William Morris is, mind you, a place where poetry is revered. Otherwise, why do you think it'd have that name? Do you know who William Morris was? No one knows. But he was an English poet. That's no small matter, ladies and gentlemen. A man from the land of John Bull. He translated the Odyssey and the Aeneid. He had the misfortune of dying in 1896. Otherwise, he'd be here with us, here in the pizzeria La Rueda, the antisubversive pizzeria, eating a luscious slice of focaccia, the specialty of the house, and washing it down with some of our exquisite quality reds, like a Termidor or a Casa de Troya or even—why not?—a Viejo Tomba, the top of the line.*

Going back to Fernando, whatever he's come to do in this pizzeria is going to be left undone. And all because of a lack of caution, something stupid, an excess of confidence. Because the fat man at the counter could have done many things. First of all, he could have not recognized him. Second, if he did recognize him, he could have been cagey, giving in to his fears and keeping his peace. Pudding for table three. A bottle of Crespi. A large pizza with ham and red pepper for table six. Innocent-like, business as usual, free of danger. In the third place, he could recognize him and make the newspapers. Grab the phone, be brave enough to do it, and call the police. What's wrong with the fat man? Isn't he a Peronista? Isn't he happy over Aramburu's death? Isn't he proud of the guy who did him in? The one who took out the gunman of the Libertadora coup, the unyielding pursuer of Peronismo and the Peronistas? Was he dying with envy over Fernando Abal Medina? A pizza man in William Morris, a man of the people who owned a neighborhood business in an area of workers, someone who could be a police informant, who could turn in the man of courage who made the Peronista masses happy, made them happy in the midst of bitterness and salaries that always fell short and endless restrictions? Just wait and see: yes, the fat man is about to turn into a snitch. There's no two ways about it, there's fascists everywhere. Even in a crappy pizzeria. But make no mistake: the fat man is the boss. And in this country the minute any poor jerk becomes the boss, he turns into a traitor, a snitch; he hates his own people and wants to get ahead, be a gentleman, made fun of in the drawing rooms of the upper classes. But he wants to get there. Besides, the poster the police put up was crap—cheap, but clear. Clearer, as Fernando is about to discover, than he thinks it is. In July of that year, 1970, a month after the death of Aramburu, they put it up all over the city. They, the Montoneros, who had killed the leader of the fascist homeland, the one who gave birth to this country, the hero of Decree no. 4161, were famous. Fernando, Pepe, and Gaby. The poster that was all over the place announced them:

WANTED FOR THE KIDNAPPING OF THE HONORABLE
LIEUTENANT GENERAL DON PEDRO EUGENIO ARAMBURU,
THERE IS A WARRANT FOR THE ARREST OF
Esther Norma Arrostito, alias "Gaby"
Mario Eduardo Firmenich, alias "Manuel"
Fernando Abal Medina, alias "Fernando"

TURN THEM IN

Did it make any sense to analyze this piece of tripe? Aramburu couldn't have been given more honorifics. "Honorable" was more than enough. "Lieutenant General" was correct and the only one that should have been used. What took the cake was the "Don." Aramburu was "Honorable" and "Don" in addition to "Lieutenant General." The height of respectability. The man of institutional, democratic, republican Argentina. The others, the Montoneros, the ones who did him in, were identified, because they were delinquents, with the humiliating "alias." Alias "Gaby." Alias "Manuel." Alias "Fernando." Fernando wasn't Fernando's alias. It was his legitimate name. Why not say the Honorable Lieutenant General Don Pedro Eugenio Aramburu, alias "the Basque"? No, only lowlifes have aliases. The good guys don't have aliases. But the poster circulated throughout the country. And the photos were not as Fernando thought them: cheap, fuzzy, and unintelligible. His mother and anyone who knew him would have recognized him immediately. "That's Fernando Abal Medina. No doubt about it, that skinny face, those eyebrows, that strong, chiseled nose, that slender mouth, that determined look. The kind of guy who's always sure of himself without a doubt in his mind, who jumps into the pool without giving it a second thought. That one, no mistake, can only be the face of Fernando Abal Medina." We know that the fat man behind the counter has now recognized him. We can guess he's afraid. But wanting to make a name for himself is enough to give him the courage to overcome his fear and turn them in. "Get over here right away. They're here." . . . "Am I sure it's him? It's him." . . . "Is he armed? How do I know? Now you want me to frisk him?"

"We're on our way right now. If he tries to leave, strike up a conversation."

The fat man hangs up. There, it's done. Nothing to do now but wait. Fernando suspects nothing, can guess nothing, since he doesn't believe in bad luck or in the snares of reality. Something dangerous happened to him after the death of Aramburu. Nothing can make him think he's in danger. Or worse, danger has nothing to do with him. They can't kill him. History is at a standstill. He cannot die. He's twenty-three years old. Who hasn't felt immortal at that age? Besides, the importance of the crime in Timote will protect him. History demands the unfolding of his life. He must explain himself. His actions alone will explain him. If he dies, no one will know the hero of this victory. Because that's what it was, a victory. It's as though San Martín had died after Maipú. Impossible. That battle paved the way for the liberation of Peru. For his standoff with Bolívar. For the loss in Guayaquil. But he had to continue to live for that to happen and for him to refuse to take part in the civil wars in Argentina. That explained him. Or he explained himself. It was necessary to know the hero of Maipú. And History gave him the time for it. To differentiate himself from Lavalle, for example. It will also give it to him, Fernando. Everyone will know he's not an assassin but a man who battles fair and square. The country must know it. He's got to go on, to denounce the regime, to bring Perón back. And when the Old Man arrives, he'll be there at his side. Right then, that's when everyone will know. The Old Man is there because Fernando did away with Aramburu. He's the one who got his hands dirty. He saved the Peronista nation from having to do it. *Here, let me do it. I'll put my hands in the shit for you. You who are workers, who have families to feed, who have no time for the shadows. Look, I did it. Here's the result. Perón is back home with his people.* Death, Fernando's sure of it, will respect him. Death has a pact with History. It won't carry off those who are still necessary. But there's something he doesn't know. It's dangerous to think you're immortal. Believing that God, History and Revolution are on your side is the surefire way to be careless about security. Living among capital letters is a lack of respect for the trivial, the small things, the vulgar everyday. What is happening to him is so insignificant that he's unaware of it. A fat man who runs a pizzeria decided to pick up the telephone, dial the number of the police, and denounce how the Revolution, History, Immortality, and the guy who kept the Peronista nation from getting its hands dirty is right there in his place—just another pizzeria that, like any other, smells of mozzarella, onions, red peppers, olives, sardines. It's not a good place for someone who, even if he doesn't believe himself to be God, isn't far from it. What is more, no one should believe that in this story Aramburu will be treated like a fascist who's against the people, that he got the death he deserved, that it was his to choose. Anyone who thinks like that is going to be surprised. Aramburu, there in the face of death, is going to show us a surprising face. From one Catholic to another he is going to talk to Fernando about the *fear of God* and, because he made the mistake of talking a lot with his victim, before killing him Fernando's hand is going to shake and the earth is going to open up in front of him. This is a tragedy we are telling. Not a story with good guys and bad guys. In a tragedy you've got to listen to everyone. Because they all have good reason to defend their actions and, therefore, their lives.

Luis Rodeiro from Córdoba sits down at their table. Nothing more is needed. Only for the police to arrive, but it's just a matter of time. Before that, it's important to know what is being said at that table. Knowing that, you know why they're in the pizzeria La Rueda, in William Morris. Almost no one knows why. Everyone who's written about the Montoneros says it's just chance, something indecipherable. The first reason is that Fernando lives nearby. Why didn't he call the meeting at his house, why take a chance, why thrash out organizational questions in a public place? But we know all about Fernando. He must have wanted to eat pizza, take a walk, get some fresh air. Was what they had to deal with so urgent? One of the questions was.

"You're drifting aimlessly," Luis Rodeiro says. "That's dangerous. Either they're going to pick you up or someone's going to end up at a relative's house and spill the beans."

The "beans" refer to La Calera, a town in the Province of Córdoba. The organization wants to show its leftist colors. It wants to say to everyone there's no mistake about it, the Montoneros are not a bunch of Catholics with a nationalist past who killed the liberal Aramburu and then begged God for pity on his soul. They're a leftist band. Like the Uruguayan Tupamaros. These guys occupied the town of Pando in 1969; the Montoneros, with Fatty Emilio Maza leading them, occupied the town of La Calera on July 1, 1970. They've got money, and they paint all the walls with slogans like "Perón or Death" and "Montoneros" and play the Peronista march for the townspeople: "In the name of that great Argentine / Who knew how to win over / The great mass of the people / Fighting capitalism." If that had been Perón in 1945, in the age of Third World revolutions, they had to turn him into a second Castro of the Americas. They exit the town and everything goes wrong. One of the cars breaks down. They take flight but the police know where to find them. Bullets fly every which way. The police open fire. The Montoneros return their fire. But two basic squads from the Córdoba Group (the heart of the takeover of La Calera) end up badly wounded. For one of them—Fatty Emilio Maza, the hero of the operation against Aramburu—death is not long in coming. And another one, Ignacio Vélez, takes a bullet in his spinal column. Their defeat leads to a disbanding of militants into other provinces. But most go to Buenos Aires. Where to put them? "Let's deal with this question right now,"

Fernando says. And he goes off with his companions to the La Rueda. He has Rodeiro come by because he wants to set up the Salta Group.

"There are about thirty," Blacky Sabino tells him, downing half the glass of red wine he ordered.

"You take charge," Fernando says. "But don't leave them on the loose for very long."

"What fucking bad luck with La Calera," Rodeiro comments.

"Tell me something I don't know," Blacky Sabino says. He looks at Fernando. "And you're putting him in charge of the Salta Group?"

"Yes."

"Someone from Córdoba doesn't know how to lead anyone from Salta."

"Where'd you come up with that?" Rodeiro asks.

"It's a joke."

"Hey, change the subject to soccer," Fernando says. "A policeman has just walked in."

"Pelé didn't make the greatest play in the World Cup," Blacky says.

"If it wasn't Pelé, who was it?" Rodeiro asks.

"The English goalie, friend," Blacky adds.

"Yes, but the head shot belonged to Pelé," Rodeiro says.

"What the hell does that matter? Pelé's head shot was masterful. But that doesn't make Pelé great. It makes Banks's block all the more incredible. There's not a goalkeeper in the world that can stop that ball. Pelé bounced it with a full sweep of his head, into the farthest corner of the goal. The guy takes flight and knocks it out. That was the greatest part about the World Cup,"

Blacky affirms. The police see them and walk over to their table. Three plainclothesmen. There are other possibilities. They could all be wearing uniforms. Or two plainclothesmen and one in uniform. Let's just say that the three were plainclothesmen and Fernando could smell them the minute they walked through the door. "No, let me put it differently, hold on. There was another goalie who could have knocked the ball out. It must have been Cejas," Blacky says. Rodeiro hesitates. But he doesn't say anything. His convictions aren't strong enough to deny what Blacky has said. Cejas, goalie for Racing, was one of the greats. Even Pelé, once the World Cup was over, took him to the Santos Club. It's as though he said, "Of all the goalies I saw in the World Cup, there's no one better than this Argentine who didn't make the cut." Because Cejas couldn't be in Mexico. It was a shame Argentina did not qualify in 1968. Blacky Sabino doesn't waste any time. He puts his hand on his .45. Fernando stops him with an imperceptible movement. One so precise that only Blacky could see it. His gesture says, "Hold on. I'll take care of this." Blacky puts his gun away. Luis Rodeiro stabs an olive, a big deal under the circumstances. It's never easy to stab an olive, and even less so if the police have come looking for you and you belong to the Montoneros organization. But he stabs it and puts it in his mouth and chews it and even spits out the pit, hitting the very center of the ashtray.

"Good evening. May I see your IDs, please?"

It's the police, two of them. The third stood guarding the door. Let's try to frame the situation.

Sitting at a table next to the window inside La Rueda are Fernando Abal Medina, Blacky Sabino Navarro, and Luis Rodeiro.

Standing guard—who seems not to have been productive—there's Carlos Ramus, in a blood-red Peugeot 404, a lovely color for a car like that. Not everyone had a 404 in 1970. A little ways away in a white Fiat 1500, looking a little muddy like all the cars of that color which seem to get dirty from nothing, is Carlos Capuano Martínez from the Córdoba Group, like Fatty Maza, who, as we have seen, is eliminated after La Calera—and like Ignacio Vélez, who ends up with an ugly wound in his spinal column, as though it could be any other kind of wound but ugly. Charly Capuano has something in common with Blacky Sabino. He's swarthy, speaks slowly, and rarely gets upset. Calmness is really what defines his gestures. They call him Skinny. Today he gets away. But, perhaps illogically, he is later killed in a similar situation. That happens on August 16, 1972, in a bar in Barracas. He's with two other companions, sitting calmly at a table, likely drinking a cup of coffee and smoking a cigarette. Two plainclothesmen enter and one stays outside, just like in William Morris. Charly Capuano's companions show their IDs. But he has already been marked. He orders his two companions to flee, takes out his gun and empties it at the two plainclothesmen. He almost kills one of them, missing by a hair. In any event, the guy falls to the ground with a scream and lies there defenseless. The bar turns into a scene from hell. Everyone screams and falls to the floor. Bottles shatter. Capuano escapes out the back door. He has a car in the street. If he gets in, he escapes. He runs off, hearing them running after him. He must go on fighting. He turns around and fires again. He kills a lieutenant captain. Capuano must have been a good shot. He opens the car door, jumps in, and roars off. But in order to get in he has to turn his back to his pursuers—who, all of a sudden, have multiplied. They fill him with lead. They write poems to him in Córdoba: "You went down fighting, Skinny, which is how one ought to die." That's Charly Capuano Martínez and he's in that white Fiat 1500. Today, in the town of William Morris.

"I've got something better to give you, officer," Fernando says. And he shows him a carefully made police badge just for these occasions. The policeman looks at it and nods.

He just says dryly, "Good evening."

He hands the badge to Fernando. He walks toward the exit. And then all hell breaks loose. It comes from the street.

The policeman standing by the door exits and joins the one on the outside. They walk toward Ramus. From three to five feet away they ask to see his ID. Ramus draws his gun and fires at them randomly, furiously but very nervously. Not taking aim. The police respond. The two on the inside—let's be clear we mean the two inside the pizzeria, one of whom asked Fernando and his companions for their IDs—escape toward a nearby building under construction. Taking up positions, they open fire. Ramus plays his trump card. He has a grenade. He takes it out and takes aim at the policemen. Too late and poorly aimed, the grenade explodes in his hand. There were few witnesses that evening. But they swear they never heard anyone scream in worse pain. They would never have believed that something could burst forth from someone's hand that way. They couldn't believe it—nor would they ever believe it—because a grenade had never before exploded in their hands, taking with it half a living body. Only unlucky lives, the kind that live on the edge, the ones that go for extremes, could end so horribly. Not always. Living on the edge can also lead to triumph, glory, myth. That's the way it is: all or nothing. That night it was nothing for Charly Ramus.

Leaning against the window, after moving the table, Fernando and Blacky Sabino return fire. There are four cops. They fire every bullet they have at the window of the pizzeria La Rueda. Rodeiro is unarmed. There's nothing for him to do. From where he is, Capuano is unable to open another round of fire. Fernando and Blacky continue to fire their guns until they realize that they've got to go for broke.

"Blacky," Fernando says, "in less than five minutes a hundred cops are going to come to back up the ones here. Either we leave now or we never leave at all."

Why didn't they escape out the back? Let us assume that they are afraid of the back. They don't know where it leads. Or if it even goes anywhere. Or whether there's an exit. They might wind up in a dead end.

They move toward the exit. They reload their guns. They kick the door out and exit shooting. A gush of blood bursts forth from Fernando's chest. He falls heavily on the sidewalk. When he sees this, Blacky Sabino runs into a house, the one next to the pizzeria. He runs toward the back and tries to jump the cement wall. The wall is filled with broken glass along the top. In the '70s they used to put glass in cement. This protected the houses. Glass from Coca-Cola bottles, Pangara wine, Fanta, Paso del Toro, 7-Up. In order to climb over, Blacky grabs the top of the wall and the glass slashes his hands. Badly wounded, he still manages to escape.

In the middle of the disaster, Capuano gets into the Fiat and escapes. Luis Rodeiro is unarmed. He gives up. Fernando is lying face down, dead. A patrol car pulls up. A door opens and a black boot appears. It's pointed and gleams with the careful work of a shoeshine boy who has produced powerful glints, so powerful that they seem to jab the night. A lieutenant captain gets out. It's unusual for a subcomissary to wear boots. But this one does. He's not just anyone. He is an imposing type, almost seven feet tall—perhaps a little less, but not by much. He has bushy eyebrows, a well-trimmed moustache, thick lips, and an aggressive nose, like a deadly bird of prey. He takes up an enormous space in reality or at least that's the imposing impression he gives. People move aside for him. Otherwise he'll just plow through them. He's the chief. He says, "Let me take a look at him."

One of the plainclothesmen uses his foot to turn Fernando over on his back. The subcomissary studies him for a long time. No one speaks. Finally, he says, "Shit, he's just a kid. A punk. As far as I'm concerned, Perón's all fucked up if he expected anything from these schoolboys." He sighs disgustedly. He doesn't like his job. At least he doesn't like the job he got today. He says, almost sadly, "Poor kid, to end up dead this way. Like a dog. And for nothing." He turns away brusquely. He wants to forget the matter. He's angry, upset in a way that surprises him. It almost sounds like he's in pain when he orders, "Take him to the morgue. You know, the Institute of Surgery in Haedo."

With his black and shiny boot, as if kicking him, he grumpily turns the body back over. Who is he? His name is Amengual. They call him the Sinister One. He's a hardass. A cruel cop, a "regrettably celebrated" torturer, as Rodolfo Ortega Peña would describe him years later. Something strange has happened to him today. The body of this kid who died fighting awakened something new in him. Pity for Fernando and also for himself. He knew he would spend the rest of his days killing punks like this who pop up one after another, multiplying until they are a plague. And each time he'd have to kill more to control them. To control everything. The state. The army. The police. The Church of Christ. Private property. The lives of citizens, especially the ones these kids were determined to wipe off the map: the big wigs, the landowners, the leaders of the Rural Society, IDEA financiers, managers of the multinationals, all of them. The entire country, damn it. *How many am I going to have to kill, torture, skin alive so the country is protected? To save it from foreign ideologies, especially atheistic Marxism, to preserve a lifestyle, its proud, never vanquished flag, so it will continue being like it's always been?*

He spits furiously to the side and climbs into the patrol car.

"Drive off," he says.

He disappears into the shadows of a moonless night. There are only dark clouds that forecast rain. Fernando's blood has flowed copiously out along the sidewalk toward the street. It reaches the edge of the sidewalk and stops there. It hesitates as though doing a balancing act. First it seems it will overflow into the street and then it seems it won't. Another bubble comes along and then the blood flows over into the gutter. It mixes with the wet mud, the dry leaves, and the balls of old newspapers—snaking along its course until it reaches a drain and disappears as it falls into the abyss.

One thing is certain from the start: el General usually leaves
his house around 11:00 AM. But not always. Which proves there
are no absolute certainties. Except to kidnap him, but that
certainty belongs to them. The rest, reality, offers no guarantees
of any kind. Everything is a risk, unstable ground. Sometimes
the general emerges; sometimes he does not. The result is that
it would be chancy to trap him on the street. It is not advisable
to leave things to chance. You've got to work with sure things,
things that have the regularity of the stars. Today he left his
house. Tomorrow, who knows? They see him from the window
across the way, from a reading room, perhaps a library that's part
of Champagnat College. The general strolls calmly, in no hurry.
He's wrapped up in a lot of dealing and has a lot of plans. He's
in the center of national politics, a center that is opaque because
it is secret, conspiratorial. He wants Onganía out. He's a bum-
bling corporativist, a latter-day Franco, someone who fails to
understand. But the general, he understands. It is imperative to
negotiate seriously with the Peronistas. The scheme to exclude
and marginalize them from the political game has got to stop.
It no longer works. He attempted it at first, in 1955, when he
expelled Lonardi because he respected the Peronistas too much
and wanted to integrate them from the outset. *Neither conquerors*

nor the conquered. He was a fool, a weak man, a Catholic nationalist with the soul of an ingenuous altarboy. These nationalists
know only how to make a bunch of noise and provoke uprisings.
In 1955 all that would work was a heavy hand. Or that's how he
saw it.

There must be some way to counter the Peronistas in this shitty
country, he told himself with rancor, anger, and a thirst for
revenge. *If the June bombardment didn't do it, nor the September*
coup, you had to find another way. Keep hitting them hard where it
hurts. Hide Eva Perón's body on them, so they'd never see her again.
If you don't, there'll be nothing but disaster. Wherever we put her,
they'll go in droves to worship her. Just like the Deceased Correa
Woman cult. No, the deceased Evita here in the country, never.
Get rid of her. Put her anywhere in the world. Not here. No one
could fault the general for the effort he was making to de-Peronize
the country. All in vain. The country was obstinate in being Peronis-
ta. He, who had taken de-Peronismo to the extreme of death, who
had General Valle shot in a penitentiary, who refused to receive
his widow, who had her told he was sleeping—he, who ordered or
accepted without batting an eye the clandestine assassinations, now
wants to negotiate and talk with his enemies. It's all that remains
and the only thing that will work without a doubt. Clearly and with
utmost caution, I'll tell this first to the union people and the demo-
cratic politicians, the conciliatory ones: there will soon be elections
and you can be candidates. And if you win you'll have what you
won. And if it's the Government, then it'll be the Government. And
if you want to bring Perón back, we'll talk. Everything is possible.
But done calmly. Everyone pulling in the same direction, toward
Argentine democracy and institutionalization.

It doesn't even seem paradoxical to the general that he's the one leading all this. History, as he is accustomed to confessing to himself, changes us all. *It must have done something to Perón. Exactly what it did to him was to change him. He can't be the same. If he, a hard-headed Basque, was able to banish old hatreds from his heart, why can't the man who lives in Puerta de Hierro do the same? After all, the years do not go by in vain and Perón has certainly lived enough years. He looks old, tired. It's as though only hatred or the desire for revenge kept him standing, lucid. If we give in to him on a few things, he'll calm down. We'll let him have his uniform back. We'll promote him to lieutenant general. There's got to be nothing more painful for a man of arms than being stripped of his rank and the absence of the fatherland he's spent his life defending or swore to defend. We'll give him back his uniform and that'll be enough: he's on our side. Now, go on and calm the country down. Put yourself on the side of people of honor.*

The general proudly believes that his task is that of the true statesman—or, better, that of the patriot. The gesture of extending a hand to his old enemy and looking beyond the horizon of dying, fading rancors is one of greatness. Will Perón be up to it? If he isn't, he will be left with something else: the weariness of the years, the desire to sit back. *The war is over. Come on, you're once more one of us. One of the nation's military men. Put up one of your own as a candidate and be done with it. If you win, you win. Not you, we won't let it be you. No, not you as President. Believe me, we're doing you a favor. Power is exhausting. We'll give you whatever you want, whatever you ask for, but not the presidency. I can't. There's a lot I can do, but I can't do everything. No one can. Not even you could. But I give you my word: Onganía is out. He's*

*the stumbling block, people like him. You know them well. They're
the ones called right-wing guerrillas. They can't even stand to hear
your name. They haven't changed. I have. I'm the man this country needs. You're the other one. Yesterday's rabid enemies, today we
stand together and we're going to find a way out of this labyrinth
that has been suffocating us for the past fifteen years. You have
my word as a gentleman and as a soldier. But I want yours, too,
Perón. Or, if you prefer, and I know you do, General Perón. None
of this business about an organized community, republicanism. The
Justicialista Party, if it comes into the system, will come in as a party
of the system, that's clear, right? Put a brake on the strong union
people, the rebellious priests, the guerrillas that go about invoking
your name and the ones that don't. We're just in time. We can do it
without much bloodshed. None of this business about a Peronista
Movement. The country needs a democratic Justicialista Party if it
wants to compete in the elections. I'll go up with my own party, the
UDELPA. If I win, I win. If not, I'll be happy to have been the one
who finally brought order to the republic.*

He's now returned home. He has no idea that he's being watched. Right now, from the reading room of the Champagnat. If he had known it, he would probably have thought we were soft, easy clay in the hands of history that we think we are making and that has surprises, frightening things, in store for us. You think you are the creator of new, never-before-imagined events. The patriot has taken the country's history first one way and then another. The providential man. The man who yesterday threw Peronismo out and who today will bring it back to everyone's benefit. But he doesn't know it. He doesn't know anything. He allows himself to be carried along by his thoughts; he has hundreds of ideas, projects. He sees a country of unity, civilian peace, and progress. A country made possible by his sincere, honest patriotism. He has, he thinks, everything under control, the perfect plan—one that can't fail, one that will carve for him the statue that he undoubtedly deserves. But there is only one thing he doesn't know. He doesn't know that they are watching him from the sidewalk across the street. He doesn't know that pretty soon they will kill him. Not to know this is not to know a thing. That's the way life is, so unpredictable that it's scary.

The young people watch him go into the building. There, where he lives. They still don't know where to kidnap him or how. They know they're going to do it, no matter what. They take notes. They call this "external fact gathering." No one bothers them. The reading room or library is deserted, at best a place in which someone appears distracted to find a book and leave. They gather facts, also, from Avenue Santa Fe. One or two persons from the organization cover the area. Let's just say that we don't have to worry about them. They will not take part in the kidnapping. They will not travel to Timote. All they do is wander along Avenue Santa Fe, mingling with people and sweeping their gaze from one side to the other without seeing anything worthy of note, anything indicating danger or anything out of place. There's a corporal there, overweight and blond. That should have caught their attention. Blond. But the guy looked insignificant, nothing more than a simple recruit, a corporal. Everything looks easy. The weight of the job (what must *essentially* be done to carry out the surprising deed they have set for themselves) is undertaken from the Champagnat. Inside there, Fernando Abal Medina follows the serene footsteps of the great founding father of anti-Peronista Argentina.

"He looks ordinary," he says. A good neighbor going out for a short walk. Is that what his doctor told him? "It's good to go for a stroll, General. A military man who doesn't die in battle dies from sedentariness. Take care of yourself." What an innocent soul he seems to be. He takes in the day. A beautiful autumn day, he can feel it on his face, the sun on his forehead. Not even a bird craps on him. Content, at peace with life. It hurts to see him that way. So exposed. He hasn't got a clue. He could be dead in a day or two and there he is enjoying the autumn breeze and the gentle sun, taking it easy.

Let's say that that day Gaby is with them. Why not? They're not going to waste her. Gaby is older than the lot of them. For example, she's seven years older than Fernando. She's been his partner for two years. But not a word about this just yet. Arrostito, who's Gaby or Skinny, approaches the window. She looks at the general.

"I don't think he's taking it easy," she says. "A guy like Aramburu never takes it easy. Or do you want to take him for a jerk?"

"Don't be smart-mouthed, Gaby."

"And don't you go feeling sorry for such a fuckup. While he's walking to the corner and back, his mind is working. He's thinking about Onganía. About how to screw him. He's thinking about Perón. The same way—how to screw him. How to present him as a peace offering and give solidity to his plans. Aren't we here because that's what he's thinking of doing? Why don't we kidnap Imaz? Because he's the real fuckup. Aramburu's not, Fernando. He's the best card the system has. He doesn't know we're here. He can't know. But don't let your guard down. When he does know it, even if we've got him tied to a bed, he'll make something up on the spot to get away and screw us. Think about that. Stow your pity. And most of all, don't think he's a jerk."

Fernando clucks his tongue in a bored fashion. "You're too smart, Gaby," he says. "I don't know if I like that."

"No one likes a smart dame. Get used to it or go fuck yourself."

Gaby drops into one of the empty chairs. She wings a leg up over the armrest and lights a cigarette. She takes a puff or two. She's a young woman. If we were to project on to her everything we now know, what was said, what was discussed, what was written, we couldn't believe it was the same person. She isn't. She still hasn't done any of the things that will turn her into the main character of so many stories, so many interpretations. Or, undoubtedly, she didn't do the main stuff. None of them did. They are only planning Aramburu's kidnapping. They haven't kidnapped him yet. And that will be the whole key. Gaby is Fernando's partner, but she knows herself to be desired by the other members of the organization, and by Firmenich most of all. He would die first before saying anything to her. He's just that proud and professional. But the others, too. Less so, but still. In any group of young bucks a woman with balls really stands out. She's up to them. She puts her life on the line like they do. She's feminine, but *weak woman* doesn't suit her. Not by a long shot. At times she goes at it with them so intently that it scares them, makes them really afraid. They all want to lay her, but she chose the chief. Fucking the chief is another one of her attributes. One of the things that make her unique, often imposing. Besides, she's attractive. And, especially, she's older than all of them. She's thirty years old. She's made it to thirty. That leads her to establish an almost maternal relationship with them, her comrades—although not always, or at least not in an excessively apparent way. But nevertheless unavoidable. Above all with Fernando. When she does it with him, the chief, when she's his mother-babe, it's that way with the rest of them. Gaby knows it and likes it. A gutsy, feisty dame, surrounded by courageous punks and revolutionary idealists. Not bad. There are many women who would envy her. Others—the bourgeois ones, the frightened ones— would shit in their panties. She has no idea of how much she will have to pay for it. The cost she will experience directly by being abused to her limits. But what she doesn't know, none of us knows. It's strange, but we don't even know what will happen to us in the next ten minutes of our lives. That's how it goes with the human condition: the principle of uncertainty in its most impeccable, most extreme expression. And perhaps its most tragic, because we live thinking it's not like that. We go on making plans, confident that we can carry them out. That's why there's a future, so we can carry them out. And if we didn't live that way, we'd be possessed by terror or madness. Gaby's learned to live without lying to herself. She believes in the revolution. But she doesn't believe in its inevitability. Everything can turn out OK. But also not OK. She usually doesn't confess this conviction that separates her from her time. A time of certainties, dreams that have to come true, a historical future that has tendered a majestic promise: the world marches toward socialism. Don't believe it. Believing that it can *also* march somewhere else makes Gaby a being apart from a certain essential sentiment of her time. She doesn't care. She won't discuss it with her comrades. She doesn't want to stand in their way, embitter their certainty of the celebration just around the corner. If they require this certainty to do what they're doing, so be it. Not her. She'll fight for the end of repression, for the national and social liberation of the fatherland, for the overthrow of capitalism, but without believing that all of this will happen because the goddess History is on their side. There is no goddess History. All there is is war. And anyone can win. The scoundrels, for example. The same ones as always. And the same ones as always did.

Let us suppose she says to Fernando, "Don't call Aramburu a *jerk* because he doesn't know we're watching him. Just because he goes for a sunny stroll and hasn't got a clue that we are planning to kidnap him. Don't go feeling superior to him because you look at him and he doesn't see you. Maybe the same thing is happening to us."

Fernando gives her a scornful look. "What's eating you? Are you trying to scare us?"

"No, sweetheart. I'm not that gone. Besides, now you scare so easy? I'm only pointing out that no one knows if he's being watched. Aramburu right now doesn't know that you're watching him. But it's too easy to feel yourself more powerful than someone else just by spying on him. And it's difficult to admit that people like us could be always being watched."

"Yeah, I know, Skinny." We've said, haven't we, that they call Gaby Skinny? She's skinny, but she's not short on a thing. She's one of those who's not skinny where you're not supposed to be skinny. She's got great, long legs. She's also long waisted, and there's an arch to it when it turns into her small but firm ass, shaped like an apple rather than a pear. "I'm going to feel superior when we've got him in Timote and we're trying him."

"That's right," Gaby concedes. "But we're not there yet."

"Not yet."

Seated at the large table in the library, Firmenich is skimming a book. He's bored. The moment of action has not yet arrived. It is Oswald Spengler's *Decline and Fall of the West*. Two blessed volumes. Spengler was born in 1880 and died in 1936. It's strange: he didn't have much of a commitment to Nazism. Almost none. Well, that's his problem. He stands up and puts the volumes back on the shelf. He steps back and looks around the library. Damn, what a lot of books. You could spend your life reading them. As far as he's concerned, he is a bit of a rustic, with only a privileged memory that allows him and will allow him to pass his courses and finish degrees with accolades and diplomas full of high-sounding words; he could read quite a bit in a couple of months. But no more. He lacks, although not fully, a special talent Fernando has in excess: the ability to reason. One could read five hundred books, but if you can't find the hidden plot, the one lurking within that connects them all, it's as though you hadn't read one.

He continues to stare at the library. Jack London, *The Sea Wolf.* Melville, *Moby-Dick.* Too many pages for only the story of a peg leg chasing a whale. Besides, he saw the movie starring Gregory Peck when he was a child. Good or bad, the story's all there, period. In the end, the captain and the whale die together. Shit, what a surprise: you'd figured that out from the start. Kafka, *The Metamorphosis.* The story of Gregory Samsa, who turns into a cockroach. What the hell did that mean? Unquestionably he'd read Oesterheld. First, in *Misterix,* and then in the novels of Editorial Frontera: *Death in the Desert, Gold Tchatoga, The Specters of Fort Vance.* Sergeant Kirk is a desertor. But even though he knows he won't return, Colonel Dodge says, "He's the most man I've known during twenty-five years on the frontier." Something like that. Is it really twenty-five? Does it matter? Kirk runs off with other rebels like himself. The gunman Shorty, former cattle-rustler. Dr. Forbes, wise, serene, the one who brings some sort of order to the excessive passions of those giants of the desert. And the young Indian Maha, who calls Kirk Wahtee because he's his *kuyanka,* something like his blood brother. Where are those men off to, drawn by chance, danger, and the disdain for bourgeois

society—capitalist progress that is destroying the West by indus-
trializing it? They go to a ranch. And that's where they live. It's a
manly friendship. There's something no one has a shred of doubt
about: anyone would give his life for the others. The ranch where
they live, where they raise horses and sell them at a good price,
is called the Lost Box Canyon Ranch. One nightmarish stormy
night in which the wash is a torrent and there is no metaphor for
it because nothing can evoke the fear of that roar, which seems to
be otherworldly, Joe Sanders the traitor shows up. He has come
to kill Shorty. The very Shorty who, facing the campfire, has just
said there are no more adventures, that everything has become
trite, that tedium has taken life over for all eternity. Joe Sanders
shows his true face (which Shorty, who's not exactly stupid, had
already figured out) and says, "It's me, Shorty. Joe Sanders. The
man who swore to kill you."

"I know, Joe. I've been waiting for you all these years. Now,
when I kill you, I'll have nothing to wait for." And then they exit
the ranch to shoot it out to the end in the torrential rain. Shorty
draws first and kills Joe. Later, he takes his place again beside the
fire. Dr. Forbes asks him, "What were you saying, Shorty?"

"Beg pardon, doctor?"

"That stuff about adventures. That they were dead. Wasn't
this an adventure?"

Shorty, dismissing the matter, shrugs his shoulders. "Doctor, since when is it an adventure to delouse yourself?" Neither
Firmenich nor many of the kids of his generation had a better
storyteller than Oesterheld. That's why they chose him: he was
the one who most moved them, who awoke in them the greatest
passions for adventure, friendship, bravery, the one who awoke in

them respect (rare in North American comics) not for the solitary hero, but for the man who finds heroism in the group, in the midst of others, who share in his struggles and his dreams. They preferred him to Salgari, Verne, or even Stevenson. Getting back to Firmenich, we will allow ourselves a conjecture: let us mistrust his passion or his sensitivity as regards reading Oesterheld. A memorist not only is unable to reason, he is also unable to become emotional. Perhaps we are seeing him from the present, knowing many—too many things—about his subsequent life. Yet not really. A memorist retains everything, allowing nothing to get lost. He privileges nothing until he can trap an unfathomable vision of a complex of events no one but he can grasp. Then he makes his decision. He might be a good strategist because he accumulates so much that his selection is exercised on the basis of a mound of an almost impossible, almost infinite mound of facts. So many facts could produce vertigo and he might make a bad choice. That's something different. But the memorist is closer to technique than to the subtle art of thinking, that precise mechanism that sensitivity affords. The man of passion chooses. He never achieves totality because something along the way always interrupts him. Passion will not wait, cannot contain itself; it cannot and will not. It's that simple. Why go on? This is my wife. This is my friend. This is my cause. I don't want to see all the rest that might exist. The infinity of possibilities will only succeed in making me dizzy, chilling me. I'll stay right here with this struggle, this battle, this woman, these sidekicks—with Kirk, Shorty, Maha, Dr. Forbes. The kids at the National School in Buenos Aires, in Avellaneda, Roca, devoured *The Ethernant* when it came out. Without a doubt so did Fernando Abal Medina, and that's why we think we have the right to say so. To deal with this matter. The Generation of 1970 (of which these boys who are waiting to descend on Aramburu are a part of) cut their teeth reading Oesterheld even before they read Verne and Salgari. We said it once and we'll say it again, as it bears repeating. Reading *The Ethernant* made you into an adult—same as reading *Zero Hour, Frontier,* and *The Ballad of the Three Dead Men.* As an epitome of tragedy, the beloved Old Man, who was without a doubt of the greatest storytellers from this country and the whole West, damn it, the one who filled the young souls of so many kids with heroes of flesh and blood with masterfully constructed stories that were drawn by the likes of Hugo Pratt and Solano López, was killed by the military goons in the ESMA prison. They killed him when he was about seventy years old. Probably this isn't the place to have told that story. It makes the story less dry. Detective novels shouldn't stray. They say what they have to say and don't get lost in reflections. What do we know? In the first place, we don't own the story. Often the story leads us. Second, more than likely we are not writing a detective story. What's there about this that makes it a detective story? Perhaps the dry, curt style. But it's not always like that. The narrative is going to take the chance with extended prayers. In turgid dialogues between Fernando and Aramburu. In the, let's say, obsessive effort to untangle some clues regarding this country. Something inevitable. The Aramburu affair is a powerful matter. One must let oneself get lost in it. Then find a way out. And then say something or a lot about what we saw in that abyss. Or say nothing. Because the protagonists said it. Or the facts did.

Firmenich is still there. Looking at the library. And he thinks the same thing all over again. *Too many books. There's too much writing. That's why intellectuals are no good for action. Always, before doing anything, they've got to read a book.*

"Tomorrow you've got to shoot yourself a cop, Raúl."

"Why?"

"What do you mean, why? Because the organization requires it. If you blow it, it's all over for you. But I can't see the motive. This is an order to you from the organization. You're not the one doing the killing. It's the order. You obey, go home and sleep peacefully."

"You make it sound easy. How do you kill a cop?"

"You take a shot of gin. Maybe two. Of course, you don't get drunk. You go out and shoot to kill. That's all. Easy as pie. You're not going to tell me you won't."

"Why a cop? A cop is a poor shmuck."

"Where'd you get that? A cop is a symbol of the regime. The soul of the regime is repression. Without repression, there is no regime. A cop is part of the system. A part of the totality of the system. When he beats the shit out of you. When he tortures you, he's not just one part. He's the totality. The entire system is that cop torturing you. There is no such thing as a cop who is not prepared to torture. Even the jerk on the corner, as though he were Snow White, all innocent enough to make you sick. It's a lie. Even he knows how to use the electric probe. If we tell you 'Bump him off,' you bump him off. When you are face to face with him, you're not face to face with a part of the system, but with the whole system. The system works through its parts. Do I have to explain this all to you?"

"Is killing just?"

"You should have asked yourself that before you joined us."

"I only asked myself that question yesterday."

"Too late."

"Kant says no. It isn't just. It means treating someone else as a means and not as a whole. You take him as a means for carrying out the revolution."

"I'm never going to ask Kant to rub a policeman out. Now listen to me good; it's the last thing I'm going to tell you. We've lived for fifteen years under dictatorships. They don't ask if it's OK to kill or not. They kill. They kill, moreover, through totalitarian regimes that are illegal and antidemocratic. That is, they don't kill—they *assassinate*. No more. We're fed up. As long as Perón is not in the country, it's an armed struggle. That's the only way we can make them bring him."

"Give me one more day to think about it."

"And what do you propose to do during that day?"

"I told you: think about it."

"There must be some book you still have to consult, right?"

"One or another."

"Ten, twenty, forty? Look, go on, read them all. No hurry, just take your time. If it takes you ten years, no problem. Then come back. But, no, hold on a minute! There's a bit of a problem. Nothing serious. I'm not sure. You tell me."

"What problem?"

"You've been with us for a month, Raúl. Why did you join up?"

"I wanted to be a theoretician. Help out that way. From my perspective. But not by killing."

"Someone told you wrong. In a revolutionary organization,

everyone does everything. Let me insist: you've been with us a month."

"So what?"

"You know too much. If you leave, you'll turn into a cop."

"I'm no policeman!"

"You will be if you leave. You're a potential stool pigeon. A privileged snitch. We're just getting started. We can't take that sort of risk."

"You're going to kill me."

"If we find someone with more balls than you, and I don't think that's going to be hard."

Right then and there, the guy gave up his books and within a week he'd killed his first cop. But Pepe, who was made of iron, did not trust them. They show up in love with theory. They don't want to know anything about actual practice. An intellectual's got to be like Cooke. It was precisely Baby who'd taught him the relationship between part and whole in Havana.

"You're something of an animal, Pepe," he told him. "But listen here. In semiology when a part comes to represent the whole it's called metonymy. But the hell with semiology. I am dialectician. Last year I read Sartre's *Critique of Dialectical Reason*. If you bite the bullet and read it, you learn to think. Take what I just told you, for example. All historical form is a totalization. But every totalization undergoes the process of detotalization because human liberty is a detotalizing nothing. As for the parts and the whole, let me make it simple for you. A cop is not a poor jerk, one more wage earner. No, there's a particular reason he became a cop. It's the system. The system becomes reality *in* him. When he demands to see your documents, you aren't seeing the system.

You're seeing the cop. The system never asks to see your documents. It asks for them through the cop. In that sense, the part represents the whole. And if that's so, it's because it forms part of a whole. Because the whole is realized through the parts and the parts make sense within the whole. If you have to off a cop, do it without any fuss. He's as guilty as Batista was."

"And we know this guy by heart," Fernando says. "We've got to act."

"There's something we don't know," Gaby says. "How come he has no bodyguard?"

"How do I know?" Fernando says. "I can't know that. I do know something: it can't be a trap. They haven't got an idea about us. There's no way they withdrew the bodyguard to trick us."

Why not take advantage of this morning walk and pick him up in the street? It would be enough to cover the back window of the automobile with a curtain and hang a suit from each of the side windows. They toss that idea. The street is always risky. You've got to take advantage of the weakness the victim presents. That weakness is that there is no bodyguard. It seems strange, but that's the way it is. The guy who shot Valle, who grabbed Evita's body out from under the nose of the people, who killed the comrades of José León Suárez, has no bodyguard. No one guards him and he asks no one to. Does he think he's invulnerable or innocent? The lack of a bodyguard decides the course of action. They will provide him with a bodyguard. They will be his bodyguard. They will guard him until he dies. But, right now, they have to guard him while they are taking him from his house. There are problems. The general lives on the eighth floor. They've got to make it there without arousing any suspicion. In the Argentina of 1970 no one aroused less suspicion than a military man. On the contrary, he aroused fear and reverence. They were running the government and they were tough. The youngster made a brilliant decision. They would go up to the eighth floor disguised as officers of the Argentine Army. They were unaware (since they were unaware of everything or almost everything) that they were going to end their career wearing army uniforms as well. But that doesn't matter *here*. If we don't tie ourselves to the event that is about to work itself out, if we don't focus our story on the kidnapping of the general, we run the risk of never finishing it. Perhaps because what happened that day and what was going to happen on succeeding days is still going on, it is a living thing. Where there is so much hatred there cannot be ashes without fire, a fire that still burns, still wounds, or kills. Valle's execution is alive in the hearts of those who will finish Aramburu off. And Aramburu's death feeds a limitless hatred on the part of Fernando Abal Medina and his associates, the authors of this crime. Not even the thousands of combatants, militants, and defenseless victims massacred by the dictatorship have managed to calm it. In turn, the crimes of the dictatorship have been so atrocious that they transcend the barriers of anything dreamed possible of men in the realm of horror. It's difficult for those wounds to close. Difficult to live with them. It's not impossible, but definitely an arduous and burdensome task. Often one that is overwhelming. But that's up to us. It is irrelevant to our story. That's not what Fernando Abal Medina and his companions were thinking about that May 29, 1970. Nor was Aramburu, that general laying his plans, seeking to create openings in History, paths that had been obstinately closed, that he himself had closed and now wanted to open in search of fresh air, a new period of risk taking and transformations. If he had changed, why couldn't the others have done so, too? The wounds of the past, no matter how serious they have been, can and must be closed—or so he thinks, steeped as he is in his error. Even though he still doesn't know it.

One of them, the one called Fatty Maza, knows how they walk, how they watch, how military men speak: he was at the military academy. Anyone who goes through a military school is marked by it. Something about being in the military sticks to him for the rest of his life. Some, for example, walk stiffly, with their butt in the air. Something else: they can never shake the habit of being early risers. Every civilian knows the saying used to characterize that unwavering military habit: early to rise, no matter what. Fatty Maza gives lessons to the companion who will go to get Aramburu on how to look, if not be, a soldier. The companion catches on quick. He's like that, quick, and hates anything slow, ponderous, drawn out, even anything complex. This defines what he is: a man of action. His name is Fernando Abal Medina, he's twenty-three years old and has a tumultuous past. It's high time we talked about him. He is the one who will take it upon himself to carry out the execution. Because on that day, Friday, May 29, the general will be kidnapped and at 7:00 AM on the morning of June 1, Fernando will point a 9 mm pistol at his chest. From about a foot away. Let's not ask ourselves if the bullet hits its target. That would be absurd.

Fernando was born in 1947. It's important to point out that he spent the first eight years under the first government of Perón. As we know, that government claimed to be opposed to all privileges except one, that of being a child. The only ones with privileges in the New Argentina are the children. Fernando spent eight years as a happy and privileged child. He is also privileged in another way: he belongs to a prosperous Catholic family. He's a student at the Colegio Nacional de Buenos Aires. He's tall, thin, with a chisled face and craggy cheekbones. He is also notably intelligent. But there is more fire, more ardor in him than reflection. Or he thinks in such a fashion that ideas become storms for him, suddenly entrapping events, and that suddenness demands action, that action that comes from a weighty mettle will almost always end up in violence. It is no accident that by the time he's fourteen years old we find him in the Tacuara Nationalist Movement. There he meets up with his companions from the Colegio Nacional de Buenos Aires: Mario Firmenich and Carlos Ramus. He met them swinging a chain at and cursing anyone who seemed unacceptable to them. If it was a Jew, all the better. If he were a commie, too. Be patriotic and kill two commies and a Jew. They'll change. Not yet. They're part of Tacuara right now. They like being bad. They're in style. Not them, Tacuara. They use gel in their hair, combed way back and flat. They meet Rodolfo Galimberti, who works briefly for the organization; he is younger than they, but also a Tacuara man who will never give up the hair gel. Who will wear leather bomber jackets like Rommel. There's a TV commercial directed at them. A commercial for Glostora, the men's hair gel of the period. There's another brand, Brancato. But Glostora not only pulled the hair back, but it also made it shine. The commercial goes this way: a young guy comes on and runs his hand happily over his flattened hair, which looks like a perfect Tacuara hairdo. A voice in off says, "Glostora, just like you like it, Juan Manuel." The name Juan Manuel evokes Juan Manuel de Rosas, a nineteenth-century strongman the Tacuara boys admire. One might think here, they're goners. They're just going to be some other gang of fascist, violent kids with chains and mitts. Jew beaters, commie baiters, fag bashers, nothing more. No—nothing in this story is linear. Presumably they will attend

secret and sinister talks by a shady priest, Julio Menvielle. Perhaps another priest, Sánchez Abelenda, is not unknown to them.
That's more improbable. We can, with coherence, infer that a
political education based on reading Maurras, Alfred Rosenberg,
and Adolf Hitler will not be adequate for the left-wing militancy
they will later undertake. The slight or nonexistent contact with
books like *Lessons of Universal History, Das Kapital, The State and
Revolution* or Antonio Gramsci's *Notebooks* must have resulted in
errors they will have to correct. Meanwhile, they are more impas-
sioned by Mussolini's *Living Dangerously* than Hegelian master/
slave dialectics, of which they are unaware and will probably
always remain unaware. They will approach Hegel by reading
Clausewitz. But in due time. That will be when they become
Peronistas. They are still part of Tacuara. They are attracted to
nationalist revisionary history: the Irazusta brothers, Ernesto
Palacio, José María Rosa, Carlos Ibarguren, Ricardo Font Ez-
curra. Jauretche, too, but Jauretche is something different. They
may have perceived in him, in his playful, lacerating and always
polemical prose the turbulent, proletarian, overwhelmingly true
taste of Peronismo.

Nevertheless, the revisionists will know how to awaken in
them the love for a fatherland that has always been yoked to the
interests of the British Empire. Sold out by enemies from within.
The commercial bourgeoisie in Buenos Aires, the enlighted op-
ponents of Rosas, the cattle baron enemies of Juan Manuel. Of
course, they are not ignorant of Manuel Gálvez. They read his
novels—especially *The Gaucho from Los Cerrillos.* Or *Time of
Hate and Anxiety.* Or *The City Painted Red.* And even *That's How
Don Manuel Fell.* They read avidly the biographer of the great

restorer Rosas that Gálvez published with such commitment in the 1930s so it could be read by laborers and office workers. And read it they did, buying out the printing. The country has lived subjected to Masonic liberalism. The May Revolution left it in England's hands. Rivadavia left it in debt. Facundo, the Tiger of the Plains, rose up in arms from the heartland, the Province of La Rioja. He was defeated by General Paz, a fifth-column general educated in Europe, a specialist on Napoleon's battles. The men in black cassocks, the devils who defended a central government, banished Dorrego in 1828 with the troops that Lavalle brings from the war with Brazil. San Martín's liberating army was placed at the service of the Anglo-Argentines! It took up the dark, sad role of internal politics. The great crime then took place: Dorrego's execution by firing squad. In Navarro, Lavalle—advised by Juan Cruz Varela, Salvador María del Carril, and the priest Julián Segundo de Agüero—killed the glorious colonel of the people, the leader of provincial rights, Manuel Dorrego, a holy man.

The vengeful figure of Don Juan Manuel de Rosas arose from this tragedy. He governed the country for twenty-two years, 1830–52, with a ferocious hand. During these years, the fatherland was free. Don Juan Manuel defended it from the villainies of the centralists and the attacks of the British and the French. He created the Mazorca, a group of gauchos skillful at slitting throats and introducing corncobs in the delicate and tight anuses of the centralists, who shit in French but begged for mercy in Spanish. Finally, Don Juan Manuel fought his most glorious battle. On November 20, 1847, he went up against the English invader, the purest expression of imperialism. The Restorer put chains across the Paraná River to keep the foreigners from getting their cargo to Paraguay. It was the battle of sovereignty. General Mansilla forged his defense in the Obligado Bend. At 8:30 the morning of the battle, he espied the enemy fleet and delivered a harangue that will ring forever in the soul of Argentine nationalism: "There they go! Consider the insult to the sovereignty of our fatherland by navigating, with no other right than force, the waters of a river that flows through the territory of our country. But they will not achieve it with impunity." Just a little before, Mansilla had muttered arrogantly and truculently, "An enemy unable to do a night's gallop thinks he's going to defeat us!"

All this fed the swagger of the Tacuara kids. They were very young and very dangerous. They hit hard. They were wont to yell, "Mazorca, Mazorca, Jews to the gallows!" But immigration was the second affront to the fatherland, which filled up with Dagos, Spiks, and Jews. Purity was lost. The country continued its trafficking or it was devoured by scum from across the sea. That drove the two-fisted whelps, violent enemies of communists and Jews, into a frenzy of upper-class xenophobia. Julio Menvielle continued to fill their heads with poison. And as though more were needed, there was Jordán Bruno Genta. They admired Primo de Rivera. They dominated the School of Law union. One night they invaded the school's cantina, shouting, "Long live General Valle, General Cogorno, and General Tanco!" They swung their chains at one and all. And even a young woman who had nothing to do with the goings-on was shot.

Their cheering for Valle, Cogorno, and Tanco shows how close they were to Peronismo. But what Peronismo do they want? One forged by Genta and Valle? We must be careful not to get Fernando too involved in all this. He was very young. Firmenich,

Ramus, and Galimberti were, too. But that's where they get their start. The founder of Tacuara is a guy called Joe Baxter. It's enough just to see the most widely published of his photos not to have any sympathy for him: he looks out at you with a sneer, proud and disdainful, like only a bad egg could. He dies on a plane trip. In the seventies, he and Galimberti would have been too much together. But in this fascist anti-imperialism the best of them, those with real talent, would go on to look for a more solid ideology, unaligned with racism, establishing a difference between the fatherland and the ranch (something oligarchic nationalism never did) and seeking real people among the workers, the classes subjected to capitalist exploitation. Before long the horizon was Cuba. And they spoke more of Juan Domingo Perón than of Rosas.

Fernando must have known the priest Carlos Mugica. Everything now really began to change. The Tacuara Nationalist Movement breaks off from the Tacuara Revolutionary Nationalist Movement. The demoniacal priest Menvielle becomes infuriated and creates the Nationalist Restorational Guard, which is like Tacuara or worse. Its acronym, because these things are important, was ingenious and cruel: GRN. It's a grunt. Menvielle and his Guard are rabid felines ready to hunt down communists, Jews, and Masons. Not Fernando. No one meets Carlos Mugica and remains the same. Mugica has turned Jesus and social justice into brothers. He was a man of limpid eyes; on the blond side; medium stature, not tall; intelligent; sensible. The revolution did not mean for him a shortcut to get rid of his habit. He believed that Jesus had come to bring the sword and not just the cross. Not only love, but love that expresses itself through struggle. The only love: that which leads us to love the dispossessed. He imagined a Christ like the one imagined by Evita in a text he will never know, *My Message*. He would have liked this sentence: "We must convince ourselves once and for all: the world will belong to the people if we the people decide to allow ourselves to burn with the sacred fire of fanaticism. Burn ourselves in order to burn, without listening to the siren song of the mediocre and the imbeciles who speak to us of prudence. They forget what Christ said: 'I have come to bring fire to the earth and I want nothing more than for it to burn.'"

These words would have been dizzying for Fernando. Mugica embodied them less. The essential decision of revolutionary Catholicism was not alien to him. The one that Evita expressed better than anyone else: *Burn ourselves in order to burn*. But Fernando embodied it to the end. That was his life. He was destined for it to be that way, and that's the way it was. Fernando Abal Medina burned himself in order to inflame others. Mugica passed on to him what he failed to seek in the great theorists of socialism. Because it was not enough for him to burn himself in order to burn. You've got to know how to burn yourself. And, especially, what to burn. Mugica spoke to him of the Colombian guerrilla priest Camilo Torres. He talked to him about the armed struggle. He introduced him to the Third World Priests. He talked to him of Peronismo. The Cuban Revolution. He even talked to him about John William Cooke. He pulled him away from the violent nationalism of Tacuara. And even from the splinter group, the Tacuara Revolutionary Nationalist Movement, that infuriated Menvielle so much. Carlos Mugica talked to him about the people and about love for those who are desperate. He told him that a revolutionary is not a man who hates, but a man who loves. And who loves, above all else, the people. To be a revolutionary is to love the poor, to choose for the poor. He also told him something decisive: the poor in our country are Peronistas.

Fernando is now part of Mugica's flock. Years later, Mugica will be assassinated. The information services will attempt to make accusations against the organization he founded, along with his friends (those who are about to kidnap Aramburu), Fernando and the Montoneros. They will put up posters in the business district. They contain an image of Mugica surrounded by lambs. Among the latter are wolves. There is one sentence on the poster. The sentence says, "There were wolves among your flock." Fernando would never have been able to be a wolf for Mugica. Not him nor anyone else among his friends. Mugica was probably killed by those who put up the posters around Buenos Aires. But that's later. Much later. So much so that perhaps it's better not to deal with it because it would take us too much astray. Let's make a note of this: Mugica's influence is decisive. Love before hatred. Love for the people, fight for them and even kill for them. But no killing out of hatred, kill out of an excess of love and because one has no other choice. Because an illegal country, one that is antidemocratic, which slips from a dictatorship to an obedient and illegitimate civilian government and then back to another dictatorship, suffocates its youth, who are pure of heart, and casts them into violence. They're not the guilty ones. They would not have chosen that path, the path of violence, in a free, democratic country, one without people who have been banned. They are victims, Mugica will think: Christian youths have been cast into violence by the blindness of those who govern them, by the oligarchy, by the military, by bad priests, by the insensitivity of that Church against which he will forever struggle in vain. We can now see how Fernando has prioritized Mugica's message. Because to love the people is to hate those who exploit them. And the more you love the people, the more you hate their exploiters. And the more you hate them, the more necessary it becomes to kill them.

That's why Fernando, that fall Friday afternoon, has decided to kill General Aramburu, the assassin of patriots, the military man become politician, the politician seeking a way out for the regime, the regime that exploits the poor, the regime that must be toppled, torn out at the roots. Aramburu wants to find a way out, but with the best manners possible, with political intelligence, the structure of the exploitative capitalist country. And get Perón into this vile adventure. He must be treated harshly. Fernando is free of any doubt: the executioner must be done away with. *That's the only way to save the country, to restore the country, and our dedication will make it possible. We do not want a regime that is any friendlier or with better manners. It will always be the same. It will always show its worst face whenever it has to. Put simply: we don't want any regime. We want to do away with it. We do not want exploitative capitalism in our country. We will seek another way. That way is egalitarian socialism. The way of social justice. A country free of the poor, hunger, with education for all, free from opulent bosses, without oligarchs or foreign consortia. It was possible in Cuba, so why not here? Aramburu, who sought an elightened bourgeoisie, one that would negotiate with Perón and bring him into the regime of democratic capitalism, with elections, a parliament, and politicians and unionism—which are and will always be corrupt— is our worst enemy. Because he is the cleverest one of all.*

The fact that Emilio Ángel Maza has military training is decisive. But in addition to this knowledge, he must be seen as a military man. Fernando is very young. Nevertheless, he has practiced efficiently. It turned out not to be too arduous for him to slip into the skin of a military man. Fernando, and we've got to say it once again, is the ideal partner for a woman of the operation. They call her Gaby and she is Norma Arrostito, the Montonero woman. A woman after all, who, using needle and thread, alters Fernando's uniform, which fits him too loosely. She had been a child, after all, playing with dolls, dressing them and making clothes for them, and altering her own. It's not likely she has studied sewing like the women of her day. It would be difficult to imagine her doing that. Just look at her now: stitching Fernando's clothes; she is all of seven years older than he is, and they've been together for two. (Hasn't this already been said?) She likes being older than he is. She admires Fernando's courage and ardor, her bellicose child.

Something more about him: that business about Gaby admiring him, that every now and then his ardor overflows, that is full of passion, are not the only things that distinguish him, that make him unusual, surprising as few men are or nobody is. He has other ardors. He's wild about film. He met Juan Villemot, his

French teacher, at the Colegio Nacional de Buenos Aires. They talk about film, European film most of all. Fernando is active in the Student Center, and that's where he started to manage the college's Microcinema. Villemot gives him a name: Bergman. Fernando proposes he organize a cycle. He begins to watch films. The first was *Summer with Monika*. What year would that have been? It's probable that he was in the second or third year of high school. Let's say it was 1962. Harriet Andersson blows his mind. What a woman and how beautful her body is, how daring, how free—how effortlessly and without shame she displays her body. He always sees *The Seventh Seal*. He discovers the Middle Ages. He is moved by the intolerable proximity to the divine. How is it possible to be in the presence of God, feeling yourself seen by Him for centuries? Fernando does not want to live under the burden of the gaze of God. He does not want God to judge his acts, whether He accepts them or condemns them. He does not want that sensation of panic. And he does not believe that God should assume this task nor that he deserves it. Death. He knows the eternal lament of men. Why do we die, why do we lose our loved ones? Why does God not defend us from Death, why does He leave us in its hands, why does He abandon us to its power, why did He create for us such a bitter end, one so terrifying, one all our own, one so solitary? He is full of disdain for Catholics who grumble, the cowards. Someone like him, who doesn't think about it because he is not afraid to die, could hardly complain to God about the existence of Death. He adds *Smiles of a Summer Night*. Also *Night at the Circus*. And the one that turns out to be his favorite, *Silence*. It's a miracle he can get it. It has just opened and it's a scandal in Buenos Aires. They ban it for viewers

under twenty-two. Fernando is fifteen years old. But Villemot
speaks to a friend of his who is a film buff. They manage to work
something out between them and get hold of a copy. That's how
Fernando sees it clandestinely. While it's true the film captivates
and fascinates him, and while his admiration for Bergman only
increases, he does not believe in God's silence. God listens to us,
and it is really only a matter of speaking with Him, of opening
up to Him our Christian heart. But He cannot always hear us.
We must grant Him his divine right to be distant, immersed in
Himself, lost in the abyss of the greatness of His own Creation.
Why the presumption that He hears us or speaks to us? His time,
which is not ours because it belongs to the infinite and we, terri-
fied, insignificant, mortal beings, cannot access the infinite, is too
valuable. How can we pretend to have Him dedicate any of it to
us? What is certain is that the world is plagued by injustice. But
why attribute it to Him? Why expect Him to provide us with the
solution? God gave us free will. For good. For bad. It's a matter of
choice. An authentic Catholic believes in prayer. Fernando never
felt alone in prayer. God, at times, leaves him troubled. Fernando
is not Swedish. He does not live in a frozen country. He lives on
the continent of the Cuban Revolution and is a fervent Catholic. No, Ingmar Bergman, God is not an absence. You can make
films on this basis. But that's all. God is where He should be and
whenever I seek Him, that's where you'll find Him, in His sacred
place, waiting for me, opening His arms to me. I pray to make
my way to Him. Some nights, he kneels beside his bed, rests his
hands on the cover, and speaks new, surprising words—ones he
never thought he'd say, words he had no idea were in his heart.
Prayer, in Fernando, is pure. It is not a negotiation with God. He

doesn't kneel before Him to make requests. Prayer ought to be a pure form for the expression of our happiness at being alive. Such happiness will serve us to nourish Him. When he prays, Fernando doesn't ask God to free him from his enemies, but from Evil. That He guide him without error in the choice of Good. He doesn't ask for protection for his people. Even less for himself. He can take care of his enemies by himself. Not to mention freeing himself from sin and choosing Good. Because he wants to be the one to decide from what to free himself and what to choose. The one who decides where Good is and where Evil is. And, boldly, the one to run the risk of confusing them and making a mistake. God has no reason to undertake the task of looking out for his people or for him.

"Lord, don't ever count on a complaint from me. If my fortune is adverse, it's mine alone. And if it isn't adverse, it's still mine alone. I am Your creation, not Your caretaking responsibility. I will never overwhelm You with complaints about my destiny. You, for me, are not absent, except in Your silence. Your presence is overwhelming. All that exists is its expression. Your silence is an invention of the egotism of men, as much of those who are little as those who are grand. They believe they are worth Your speaking to them. Your sparing them pain. Every egotist is a coward, thinking only of himself, asking only that nothing harm him, nothing frighten him, wishing to escape, above all else, from the fear of Death. If he hears Your voice, if You speak to him, he will go calm. That's why he questions Your silence. What kind of God does not assuage my fears, who does not address me with sweet words, who does not let me know that He is protecting me, taking care of me, and will do so until the final instant, that of the supreme fear? Those who are grand are egotists and Your silence offends them. Bergman belongs to this race, that of those who wish to speak to You as to an equal. Because they are, or believe themselves to be, gods. What kind of God is this who does not speak to me, does not deign to appear to me, who ignores me? Does He believe me to be so insignificant, does He value my talent so little, is it so easy for Him to exist without me, to not even exchange a few sentences with me, to ignore my opinion, not to know if I believe in Him or not? Unsatisfied, offended or fearful, they complain incessantly. You will never hear any reproach from me, any lamentation. Your presence and Your voice are the irrefutable fact of the life You have given me. I have no need to seek You in other landscapes. In other geographies. On the contrary, You are at times all too present. Your voice, which others do not hear, troubles me. Because I am troubled by the life that bubbles up in my blood. This life, the one You gave me, usually is too much for me, overwhelms me. What more do I need to know to believe in Your existence and to express to You my joy? Day after day, my prayers will always be for this, to express to You my gratitude for that irrefutable fact: the life that I received from Your hermetic, hidden power. I need no more. The rest is up to me. It is my liberty."

He at times thinks that the words he chooses to address God suffer from solemnity. He quickly discards this idea. God is splendid, imposing. What other language could he choose? Not the one he uses to speak with his friends or with his professors. Often in earlier years he spoke to Him in Latin. His prayers had recourse to the language of Cicero, Petronius, Horace. He finally gave up this wearisome habit. He asks himself now if he

shouldn't use the colloquial Argentine form of "you." It enter-
tains him to imagine the result: I'm praying to You in Argentine,
Lord. Because I'm an Argentine. Because I'm from Buenos Aires.
Because You'll understand me better if I speak to You in the language of Buenos Aires or because You're not going to understand
me or ever listen to me at all and You know it doesn't matter to
me. All that matters to me is to tell You what I always told You.
Whether I say it to you in Latin, in fancy Spanish, or in Buenos Aires Argentine: do not concern Yourself for me. I am Your
creation and that is enough for me to venerate You. If You wish to
remain silent, do not speak. If someone is in charge of his life, it
is You. Just forget me. I'll worry about me. Because I wish to be
free and even to fight for the freedom of others, the oppressed,
the exploited, the poor. I will never ask You why there is so much
hunger, so much misery in this world. Because I know why: it is
so full of sons of bitches. I'm going to confess something to You:
there are those who believe that You are on their side. On the
side of the sons of bitches. They pray to You in the best churches
because they have the money to build them. They believe that
to flatter You, to build cathedrals to You, is to capture Your heart.
Others believe that the powerful, by offering their wealth to You,
can ask You for Your assistance and they will receive it. Others
are even worse: not only will You help them, but that You are one
of them. That Your corporation is the Vatican. They do not understand. They do not know the truth. What You had to do, You have
already done. Now, the war is our business.

Villemot goes with him to speak to the college authorities.
Fernando requests the necessary permit in order to show the

Bergman cycle. They almost throw him out. How can he, Abal Medina, dare such a thing? Where did he get such an idea? What is he thinking? Does he want to poison his fellow students?

"What do you want me to do? Show dumb films? Hollywood films? Do you want a Doris Day cycle?"

"You are insulting us."

"And you are treating me and my fellow students like a pack of idiots."

Villemot and the illustrious Catholics in his family saved him from expulsion.

The Bergman cycle falls through. Days later, Villemot tells him, "Don't give up, Fernando. And don't take sides. Truffaut and Resnais and Godard admire Hollywood films."

"Professor, you're making fun of me."

"No, I'm proposing that we do a cycle of Westerns. You've got to see John Ford's films, Fernando. *The Searchers.*"

"I hate the Yanquis and their stupid films, professor. They're imperialist garbage. That would surely be to poison my fellow students. Cowboy pictures! Do you remember that one with Gary Cooper? The glorification of the individualist hero. A town of cowards and a valiant sheriff. You want me to show that? You want me to tell my fellow students that societies are made up of sissies? Pansies who hide in their homes at the first sign of the enemy? That only the sheriff is courageous and has the balls to face up to Evil? I'm sorry, professor. That's not for me."

Professor Villemot is a sensible man. He does not want Fernando to become entrapped in certain ideas. He would like to see him more open. Less dogmatic. Film is more than Bergman.

The Yanquis might be imperialists, and he believes a lot less in that axiom than his rebellious student, but they created film. Ah, if only he could talk to him about Billy Wilder.

"Fernando, that film you dislike so much lends itself to other readings. It was written by a great screenwriter who was persecuted by McCarthy. His name is Carl Foreman and his name is on the blacklist. The town has reasons as valid as those of the sheriff. That's why it's a tragedy. Everyone is right. The motives of everyone are valid. They must be taken into account. Do you want me to tell you what tragedy is? The fight between what is just and what is just. Don't ever forget it, Fernando. And this is only one of the dozens of possible readings of that masterpiece that lasts a scant eighty minutes. Eighty-five at the most."

"I'm sorry, professor. Maybe it has other readings. But, you know what? Mine is what is important to me. And excuse me, but I'll wipe my ass with the rest of them."

Villemot gives up.

There are problems, but they overcome them. Repairmen
from the light company or the gas company start to do some work
on Montevideo Street. They become upset. Why now? But they
waste no time in finding a place in which the pavement is not
torn up. It's all taken care of. The path to Aramburu is cleared.
They are almost not afraid, unwavering: everything will turn
out fine. They have a safe house in Villa Urquiza. That's where
they've started from today, setting out to seek their goal. That
central safe house is on the corner of Bucarelli and Ballibián.
There are some nice movie houses close by. Neighborhood movie
houses that will later be swept away by shopping center multi-
plexes. You go into a neighborhood movie house. But not into
one in a shopping center. You go into the shopping center. Once
inside you look for the movie. Villa Urquiza is a lower-middle-
class neighborhood, made up of the hardworking people who
open their shops early and who live off the credit afforded by the
cooperatives. It is near Saavedra, the neighborhood made famous
by Leopoldo Marechal. The Montoneros have a photographic
lab there. They go out in search of their prey. That Aramburu is
their prey transforms the adventure into an overwhelming act of
historicity. Let's skip some of the details. The following is what
is important: the back seat of a Peugeot 404 is occupied by Fatty

Maza in his captain's uniform and Fernando, who is wearing
the uniform of a first lieutenant, knows by heart how to talk,
how to move, and even how to think like a military man. They
have established something. An ironclad, unanimous decision: if
something goes wrong, if the whole thing sours, if they have to
die, they will die. Let's pause here. They know they can die. That
any error is enough to kill them. What brings them to accept,
assume such an extreme risk, the most extreme of all? What do
they know about Valle and those who were shot in José León
Suárez? Little. They have only read *Operation Massacre* by Walsh
and *Martyrs and Executioners* by Salvador Ferla. Is such a small
list of books enough for them to gamble their lives? Let's make it
clear: no one can say they only consulted a *few* books. There are
no others. If there are, they're in a basement somewhere, hidden.
The business about Valle and the massacre in José León Suárez,
because it is the darkest chapter in the Liberating Revolution,
has been systematically silenced by the thugs who run the country. Only two honorable persons—a Peronista, like Ferla, and a
writer who has begun to trace his powerful destiny, like Walsh—
have dared to confront the great secret crime, that crime that the
complicity of everyone, *everyone,* has condemned not to exist. But
these young people do not nourish themselves with books alone.
These young people have been wrought, carefully constructed
by fifteen years of dictatorships and military and civilian farces.
Onganía is an abominable, intolerable person. The fact that that
troglodyte is in charge of the country is an affront to the Argentine people. What is more, when he falls, after proclaiming the
death penalty, an obscure general from the United States, a mili-

tary man no one knows, will be announced on television at six in the evening. Or before. Or later. They tell the country there is a new president and the country is startled to find it out on television. That's an affront. A clumsy gesture. Authoritarian laughter from the barracks. Not only did the country not vote, but it did not choose its candidates. We'd never seen this guy's face before. The generals had elected him. That's the last straw in this banana republic. Meanwhile, the leader who called upon millions of voters remains banned. And that ban has another powerful cause: the Doctrine of National Security. A lot of things could come out of Peronismo. But since it counted on the overwhelming support of the people, the Marxist danger lurked in its bosom. And that danger, in the midst of the Cold War, was the obsession of the United States. It was the empire that also said to be careful with Perón. The poor love him too much. No matter what he thinks, he's a danger to Western democracy. Because we believe that the leaders lead the people around. But it's also the people who set the leaders on paths the latter are unwilling to pursue. Driven by the masses and fearful of losing them and in order to retain the power confided in them, they take on whatever role is necessary, and if it's Marxism, that's how it is. Even more so in a continent shaken by the Cuban Revolution. By Che Guevara and his theory about that Revolution as the vanguard of all others, the model to follow, and a history possible anywhere, in all of America. What will Perón do, shrewd as he is in dealing with the facts as they are dealt to him, facts in the majority, knowing as he does how to grab hold and make them his own? No way to know. As unknowable as it is dangerous.

The young people who climb aboard to go in search of Aramburu might wonder as they asked themselves, Isn't that a form of violence? Depriving us of our most basic political rights, isn't that a form of violence? Who was responsible for the violence, us or your hatred, the locked down country you created after the cursed events of 1955? We are on the verge of kidnapping Aramburu. But the violence doesn't begin here. Don't be asinine and stop lying. The violence began with you on June 16, 1955, when you bombed an exposed and defenseless city. And then you went on with Valle and his comrades. The ones sacrificed in the garbage dumps of José León Suárez. Felipe Vallese whom you "snuffed out" under torture. Assassins. Villains. Assassins pretending to be champions of democracy. Now hear this: today we are taking Aramburu away and we are going to subject him to Revolutionary Justice. Something you wouldn't do for Valle or the ones you slaughtered in José León Sánchez. If we find him guilty, we are going to kill him. But don't come telling us that we are responsible for the violence. He was the one. He and the whole retrograde military that massacred defenseless citizens in 1955. That's when the violence began as far as we're concerned. That's what we're going to accuse him of. He'll say they were navy planes and that he didn't know a thing. We will know how to reject that sort of weaseling. If he hopes to save himself with that, he's wrong. The September coup emerged from the June bombs. Tyranny, from that coup. With differing masks, it has been the case ever since and you have every intention of persisting in any way possible. Do not the people have the right to rise up against tyranny?

Now a very complicated point emerges here. Someone must ask the question. Someone has got to ask those twenty-three-,

twenty-two-, and twenty-one-year-olds who told them they are
the "people"? (Perhaps we're getting ahead of ourselves. It's possible, almost inevitable, that Aramburu, crafty as he is, will sub-
sequently ask them this question. But it's got to be asked here.
It's too important.) The people had their say in the rebellion in
Córdoba. But who are you? Who made you the delegates of the
people? By what sleight of hand do you appropriate something as
complex as "popular justice"? How can you incarnate the people
if the people are going to find out about Aramburu's death in
the newspapers? Was there at least a mass meeting? The people
delegated you as their representatives? Let's press the point, as
there is no reason for it to be easy. If you kill Aramburu, by what
miracle of history will it become an act of "popular justice"? No
one would think to deny that the Peronista nation hates Aramburu. But they also hate Rojas? But why not punish him, too?
Certainly, the Peronista nation does *not* know that Aramburu is
the regime's backup. Did you tell them? No, you know about it.
You are the vanguard. The vanguard always knows *more* than the
people. That's why it's the vanguard. But that "knowing" condemns the vanguard to act at the margins of the people. To distance itself from them. That distancing is dangerous. It produces
a paradoxical and often tragic result: the people do not know
what the vanguard knows; the vanguard does not know what the
people know. And since they don't know, they don't know what
they want. Did the Peronista nation want Aramburu's death? Did
they even want Rojas's, someone they hated more? Do you know
the Peronista nation, those people whom you invoke so much?
You are young people from the upper-middle class, who studied
at the Colegio Nacional de Buenos Aires, who are ultra-Catholic

and subscribe to a reactionary nationalism, who are—although you see it as a virtue and maybe to a certain extent it is—*too* young, what do you know about the Peronista nation? Undoubtedly, you know something. But is it enough to do justice in its name by killing someone? These are uncomfortable questions and they are uncomfortable because they are the ones that must be asked. They're questions with too much at stake. Let's jump ahead a bit: these young people probably do not represent the people nor do they exercise any kind of popular justice. But the act they are about to commit has been wrought by a complex historical plot. It isn't just any act, despite however we choose to refer to it. If we decide to categorize it. But that's why we chose fiction. Fiction does not judge. It is the most impeccable instrument created by man for the expression of the complexity of existence. Perhaps there exists no concept that can grasp and exhaust the crime in Timote. The Aramburu affair is the creation of an entire historical plot, of the entire development of events that converge on that May 29, 1970, and whose principal creators have been those who consider him an abomination. It was in the spirit of the times. It expresses the context in which history was taking place. Rucci's assassination is an assassination with no other reading possible. The word "assassination" expresses it completely, contains it. It takes place in a country whose major leader has been consecrated by *the people* (and here, yes, the people) with more than 60 percent of the votes. Aramburu dies a victim of stupidity, hate, the violence of his own class. He dies in the midst of a people who are fed up. In the midst of a reactionary dictatorship which is the fruit of the retrograde politics that put it in place. That politics is now fifteen years old.

Fifteen years during which Peronismo was forbidden, banned, slandered. Fifteen years of military governments or puppet civilian governments who have taken advantage of the government to benefit from the prohibition against Peronismo and its leader. What did they seek to gain? To create on their own a country that denies the voice of the majority, that mocks them, that defames their leader, that turns democracy into an abominable farce? It is creating exactly what Argentina created: the violent response of a youth fed up with politicians and lying and illegal military men. Only violence remains when tyranny pursues obstinately its own blindness.

We stop here. We will not fail to return to these complexities, to this dark and murky story. Not to one that is impenetrable, but to that *impenetrability*, which is in itself arduous and is frequently dispiriting: the more we penetrate it, the more complex it becomes, eluding for us the possibility of a *single* certainty, a *single* totalization that will put an end to the incessant detotalization. Let us continue.

There are a few minor details that add tension to the story. We ignore them, setting them aside. We are concentrating on what is essential. That which cannot help but be narrated. But, why deprive ourselves of a few things that might take place? If they add tension or not to the story is secondary and is of no importance to us. And what if they enrich it, give it substance, density? Would they not be, in that case, part of what is *essential*? Besides, what is essential? For example, a tall, loudmouthed guy might have shown up in the library, a janitor, a math teacher, a measly type with a heart of ice, part killer, part cocky.

"What are you guys doing here?" he asks in an irritated, suspicious voice.

"What's the matter?" Fernando says quickly. "Since when is this place off limits?"

"I could swear I've never seen you before."

"By the same token, we've never seen you before."

"Me? I'm a teacher here."

"We were students here and we still come around to look things up."

"There are better places."

"Not as far as we're concerned. We got our education in this school. It's like our home."

The tall, loudmouthed creep calms down.

"You're nostalgic," he says.

"Is there something wrong with that?"

"No. I am, too."

"And how do you show your nostalgia? Do you go every now and then to the brothel where you did it for the first time?"

The guy can't believe his ears.

"What did you say, you little piece of shit?"

Fernando draws a .45.

"Look, shrimp, either get out of here now or I'm going to blow your head off. And if you go to the police, I'll track you down and when I find you, you're dead meat. So keep your nose clean, kid. You walked into the lion's den like a dumb shit. If you want to save your skin, clear out, don't come back and keep your mouth shut for two years. At least."

He takes the safety off the pistol. He growls, "Scram, turd."

The shrimp disappears and is never heard from again.

We know more about Fernando than we did before. He's icy. But he's got a short fuse. When he gets mad, passion consumes him. And that's when the guns come out. He likes guns. As much as sleeping with Gaby. One might even say more. But it's not a sure thing. Let's say, more or less. Firing a shot is like fucking for him. A shot, a discharge. The shot is upsetting and the discharge burns. Like an orgasm.

Someone might say he shouldn't have been so in your face with that guy. Shouldn't, couldn't. Well, yes he could. Someone might say we have no proof. Heck, what's the matter? Does anyone have proof for anything? Someone might say he should have been more cautious. That he shouldn't have taken his gun out. What if there was no other way? Firmenich defines him as *fearless*. What does someone who is fearless do and not do? Firmenich says nothing serious happened while they were at the Champagnat. And what if this didn't strike him as serious? Let's not waste our time. As far as we're concerned the episode is realistic and jibes with what we might call Fernando's style. He flies off the handle on occasion. Loses his grip. He's icy, but excitable. Yes, the two things are possible. Nevertheless, if you prefer, we could shorten the episode, make it more realistic. Leave it for others down the road and that will strike us as even crazier, more the fruit of our imagination than reflections of reality. Let us insist: What are we talking about when we speak of reflections of reality? What reality? The one Firmenich recounts? Please, you can believe us more than you can Firmenich, more our legitimate ambition to propose realistic episodes based on our long experience as novelists than the improbable, possible, or more than possible tactical lies of Firmenich, who was not looking for the truth, nor did it matter to him to provide it, but rather a version of the facts that would give him what he needed: the prohibition of the *Peronist Cause*. He needed this prohibition to demonstate to the weak sisters who had been abandoned once the organization became clandestine that superficial militancy was impossible for the Montoneros, that clandestinity was something imposed and that there was no other route for them. "The greatest of our political errors," Roberto Perdía would say. We know who: the person who shared leadership with Firmenich. That's how Firmenich recounts the death of Aramburu in September 1974 in the organization's magazine. He will say that the story also belongs to Norma Arrostito. It comes out in the form of an interview. Nothing seems very clear. Arrostito will deny her participation. The important part is what follows: the only thing *realistic* about the tragedy in Timote is a version told by Firmenich. There is no other. As though they were unwilling to abandon a secure anchor, historians have followed it respectfully word for word. *Firmenich's word.* We propose the opposite: Firmenich's version is Firmenich's version. This alone would be enough not only to distrust it, but to find it false. There is, therefore, nothing realistic in the tragedy at Timote. The only thing realistic is fiction.

On the other hand, there are things that present us with no problems. What is most improbable about the episode with the jerk who comes into the library is that Fernando took out his .45. That exposes him too much. He gives himself away as a guy with a gun in the library. Something unusual. The jerk, if that's what he really is, rather than running away scared, goes to the police and turns them in. Let's change things. Let's say it happened this way:

"I could swear I've never seen you before."

"By the same token, we've never seen you before."

"Me? I'm a teacher here."

"We were students here and we still come around to look things up."

"There are better places."

"Not as far as we're concerned. We got our education in this school. It's like our home."

The tall, loudmouthed creep calms down.

"You're nostalgic," he says.

"Is there something wrong with that?"

"No. I am, too."

"See you around sometime."

"It's no accident. This is a lovely place to look for books. To pull them out and read them peacefully." The guys loosens up. He slowly turns around. Before leaving, he says something like a pleasantry: "I hope you find what you're looking for."

Fernando says with a winning smile, "Us, too."

The guy leaves.

Yes, possibly this is more realistic. Besides, Fernando tells the guy that they hope to find what they're looking for without bothering with any books—except, suddenly, there is one. "We're looking for a book maybe you don't remember or even know, jerkhead," he says somewhat merrily. "We're looking for *The Black Book of Tyranny.*" That book and Aramburu are one and the same.

There's a lull. Dead time. But the decision is made quickly. Fernando says, "Let's go."

They cross the street in pursuit of the right-wing gunman. Will they return? There's no denying it: everything is easy. It will not be a heroic day. No one is waiting for them when they emerge with their prey. They will not have to open fire to get through. They won't have to make their getaway from a swarm of patrol cars in hot pursuit, deafened by the sound of emergency sirens, running red lights, running over one or another pedestrian—some poor guys who didn't see them in time. Nothing like that. It's their lucky day. Things turn out as though some magic key opened all the doors for them. Any one of them might think the gods of revolution are on their side. Let's not ask ourselves who the gods of revolution are. They don't even know.

Suddenly, if we have maintained our perspective *in* the street, something incredible happens, but it's what they're there for: Aramburu steps out of the door on Montevideo Street. He's not alone, of course. Fatty Maza is with him—all buddy-buddy, with his arm around his shoulders. It even looks like he is patting him on the back like an old friend. Fernando is holding him securely by the other arm. And there's a third person, also a military man, who is with them, walking three or four steps behind. They are in no hurry. It is a warm, luminous day. Why not go out for a walk? But—hold on a moment—how did we get here? How did they get Pedro Eugenio Aramburu to leave his house?

Fernando and Fatty Maza reach the eighth floor. Fatty is a dead ringer for a military man. Fernando, not so much. But he's got a submachine gun under his jacket. No one would say he's not prepared for whatever might happen. The jacket is olive green. The other guy stays behind, as though guarding the elevator. No one knows his name. But we do. Not because we've made him up. It's just because we happen to know. He's the one who will soon end up in La Calera Prison. He's the one who'll see Fatty Maza die. The one who'll end up with a bad wound in his spinal column. His name is Ignacio Vélez. He won't last long in the Montoneros. We won't be able to put up with Firmenich's leadership. Many years later, already the twenty-first century, we listen to him say in a pastry shop on the corner of Coronel Díaz and Santa Fe, "It's too bad the one who ended up speaking for everyone else was Firmenich. I swear to you, Manolito was a blockhead. Now he's here. He stands guard outside the apartment, near the elevator."

They ring the doorbell. Aramburu's wife answers. "Yes?"

"We're army officers, ma'am. We're here to speak with the General."

She is either so very ingenuous or very trusting or so far removed from truth, so far removed from what her husband stands for and the risks he might be exposed to, that she reacts with the calm, generous amiability of a British lady. Besides, in 1970, people were more ready to open their doors than now—among other reasons, because Aramburu had not yet died.

"My husband is taking a bath. May I serve you a cup of coffee?"

The "army officers" accept. Aramburu comes out. He seems to be in a good mood. He drinks a cup of coffee with these young men in arms. He asks them something simple. She would have had to ask them.

"What are you here for? What superior gave you the order?

"You have no bodyguard, General. Our superiors thought it wasn't a good idea and sent us to take care of it. From now on, consider us your bodyguards."

Aramburu thanks them. Fatty Maza is the last one to speak. Aramburu looks at him and says, trying to be relaxed and friendly, "You're from Córdoba, aren't you?"

"Yes, General," Fatty Maza replies.

Suddenly the wife says, "I've got to go."

"Where're you going?" Aramburu asks, surprised.

"I've got some errands to run. I won't be long. I'm leaving you in good hands. You military men feel much more comfortable with each other."

The woman leaves. Neither Fernando nor Fatty Maza stand up. That should have caught Aramburu's attention. Nevertheless, he seems more worried about his wife's sudden departure. No one says a word. No one knows what to say or no one wants to say anything. They look at each other, as though each party is trying to make the other out. When she exits, the wife does not see Ignacio Vélez, who hides behind the stairs.

Fernando's face hardens. The General notices it. Concerned, he asks, "And where are you going to take up stations?"

"Wherever you say, General," Fernando says.

"I trust it will not be inside the apartment."

"If that's what you want. If you don't, however else," Maza says.

Aramburu takes a sip of his coffee. He slowly sets the cup on the table. His hand does not shake. He looks at Fernando. "Tell me, officer, how old are you?"

"Old enough."

"Old enough for what?"

"To guard you, General, of course."

"Of course," Aramburu repeats. "Why did you let my wife leave?"

"Why wouldn't we?" Maza says.

"And what if she noticed? What if she went to ask for help?"

"And why would she do that?" Maza says, innocence all over his face. "Your wife was very polite. Do you think she confused us with bad guys?"

"You . . . ," Aramburu begins to say.

Fernando stands up. He says harshly, "General, if we allowed your wife to leave, it's because we have nothing against her."

Maza looks at him in surprise: he's dropped his mask. So quickly? Wouldn't it have been better to wait a while? Wouldn't it

have been possible to get the General outside without him notic-
ing anything? No. Fernando didn't rush things. Aramburu was not
dimwitted. As soon as he asked why they let his wife leave, he let
them know he knew. They were not Argentine Army officials.

"Do you have something against me?" Aramburu asks.

"We can't say that right now," Fernando says.

Aramburu starts to take another sip of coffee.

"That's enough," Fernando says.

"I think I'm going to need a bodyguard to guard my body
against you," Aramburu says.

"It's too late. They should have given you one before we arrived."

"My patience has run out, gentlemen," Aramburu says. "What
do you want? What are you after? What do you need?"

Fernando says, "Only you, General." He opens his jacket and
takes the submachine gun out. "You're coming with us now."

"Where?"

"That's enough talking. In case you haven't noticed, we're
kidnapping you."

"You're crazy," Aramburu affirms in a hard voice.

"Our mental health is our business," Fernando says, adding,
"Is it such a surprise someone might kidnap you? First, you're
conspiring against the government. Onganía, Imaz surely know.
Second, do you think your story is all that innocent? So unlikely
to have provoked permanent hatred? You suffer from an excess of
the past, General. One can die from that."

"Which possibility have you chosen for me?"

"This is not the moment to deal with that topic. Follow me,
General. If you try anything, I'll kill you. It's that simple. Just

understand this: I'm not afraid to die in this operation. That's the first decision I made when I undertook it.

"You give little value to your life."

"My life is worth a lot."

"And you're ready to give it just to make me leave my house?"

"I'm kidnapping you, General."

"Do you plan on asking for ransom? We don't have much we can give you."

"I'm not a criminal."

"Anyone who kidnaps is."

"Don't say dumb things. Or do I have to tell you who you are? This is a political kidnapping."

"Then you'll get even less. I am a retired general. I'm sixty-seven years old. I live off my memories and I am unimportant in the current life of this country."

Fatty Maza laughs out loud.

"And, in addition, you think we're a bunch of jerks. General, we know who you are, what you are up to now, what your plans are—and, in particular, we have some questions to ask you about your past."

Fernando shows him the submachine gun.

"Look, I'm not carrying this as decoration. Either you come with us or I'll kill you right now. Understand?"

They leave.

It all seemed strange to Aramburu. They're kidnapping him? Is it so easy to kidnap him? Don't these youngsters realize the gravity of what they are doing? He is who he is, Pedro Eugenio Aramburu. He's not a politician, he's not a civilian. He is not a military man of insignificant rank and little importance. The country will explode if something happens to him. A lot of people owe him a lot. The country owes him a lot. And the country also expects a lot of him. He overthrew Perón. Everything was complicated after that. But now he's the one that can put things back in order. *I'm the military man who best understands the way out this country needs. I'm the one most prepared. The one who managed to overcome the hatred that so many keep alive. The one important person who can talk man to man with Perón. I overthrew him and I will rescue him for the country. Whether he likes it or not. We need that old man, who's an authoritarian, a fascist. He changed. I changed. He did too. What's more, I can lead him away from the temptations of the left. If we don't bring him back into the country's military, the Marxists are going to seduce him. Perón's only interested in power. He'll do anything to get it. If it has to be Marxism, which deep down he hates just as I do as a member of the Argentine military, then it will be Marxism, which is getting stronger day by day in Latin America. He could turn Argentina into*

*another Cuba. All the workers are with him. Not only that, but he
is gaining support from the most unlikely quarters: priests, young
Catholics, students, guerrillas, not to mention all his followers, who
always stayed with him. The union people, for example. We could
even buy them, despite how they live happy, sunk in corruption up
to their necks. They're Peronistas. Either we claim them or they'll go
over to international Marxism. Who else but me can prevent such
an atrocity? Is that why I'm here? Are these kids the paid assassins of
Onganía, of Imaz? Because in order for me to persuade the West to
retain Perón, I have to get rid of Onganía, who probably studied at
the School of the Americas, but who is laughable as a soldier of the
West. Does he have the courage to have me kidnapped? He's stupid,
but not completely. And what if these young men are from the army?*
That's the other side of the coin. *You want to steal Perón from us.
We want him for Marxism, and you want him for the West. And he's
the only one who can do it. Forget about continuing to live, General.
We're struggling for a cause. And our cause requires your death.*

At this point, Aramburu shudders. For the first time he's
found a motive for his death. The word *cause* makes him shake.
He knows men will do anything for it. They die and kill for it. He
knows there's nothing more dangerous than a man with a cause.
He takes a look at his kidnappers. He's bothered by the fact they
don't hide their faces. He can recognize them later. Something,
however, worries him more: one can see the pig-headedness of a
cause written on their faces. Those young men have a cause. If
that cause requires his death, he's a goner. He can only hope it
doesn't. Or convince them it doesn't.

He continues to maintain that they're military men. There
is a certain disdain in that belief. In the end he believes, as do

all military men, that civilians are a bunch of cowards. Violence frightens them. Nevertheless, what kind of military men? How did he miss it? Or hadn't any of his men told him that a new group, nationalist or Peronista or tied to Onganía's plans, had sprung up? An action group. Capable of such a thing. But every action requires the element of surprise. If they had detected them, this would not be happening. This, his kidnapping. Who are they? He doesn't even suspect it. It's not the moment to tell him. To describe to him their militancy and (in particular) the motives for this militancy. But, General, we've told you. Maybe you didn't pay attention. Or you were somewhere else, thinking about something else. Something like that. Those who lead the operation were Mario Eduardo Firmenich as a police corporal, Carlos Capuano Martínez as the chauffeur, Carlos Maguid as the priest, Ignacio Vélez and Carlos Gustavo Ramus as the civilians in the Peugeot, Fernando Luis Abal Medina as the first lieutenant, and Emilio Maza as the captain. And a woman, the only one in the group, the Montonero Esther Norma Arrostito—Gaby, to her friends.

Unlike the others, she got her start in Marxism. Nothing to do with churches or sermons from the pulpit or hosts or bowing down before the tortured man on the Cross. She read Marx, Lenin. She didn't read Hegel, but something she did read—or found things relating to her in other authors—on the basis of which she reached that conclusion that we all, sooner or later, reach: Hegel is everywhere. Or, as someone said, every age defines itself on the basis of how it reads Hegel. She read other things and saw films that changed her. She read Fanon and Sartre. That brave woman, who will have to tolerate the most terrible forms of pain without saying a word to her tormentors, knows by heart sentences by Sartre from the incendiary prologue he wrote to Fanon's book, "In the first moments of rebellion." And what are these our moments but that: the first moments of rebellion? What does Sartre say, Gaby? What must be done in these moments? "You must kill: killing the European is killing two birds with one stone, suppressing at the same time an oppressor and someone oppressed: one man is left dead and the other free." How closely allied are the destinies of Algeria and Argentina! Even their names are closely linked, signaling that their struggle is one and the same: Algeria/Argentina. Argentina suffers from internal colonialism. Also external colonialism. It is subjugated by imperialism and its local allies. That's why liberation must be both national and social. And they must occur together. They are not two stages. They are

one and the same. One must through the same struggle free himself from imperialism and from the national ruling classes that
represent it. We are part of the Third World. Our subjugation
is not colonial, like that of Algeria. In that way we are different.
Our subjugation is neocolonial. The colonizer is not within. He
has his allies on the inside, of course. His puppets have linked
their interests to imperialism. And the army that defends the
neocolonial project of subjugation. But the true colonizer, the
one who maintains the system of colonization, is the external
colonizer, the Yanquis. There is no going back, this Gaby knows.
Sartre tells her that: "Decolonization is on the march and all our
mercenaries can do is delay it." Like the soldiers of the right-wing
army. They will kill ten, they will kill a hundred. They cannot kill
History. History is on the march toward socialism and that will
bring order to the world, grievances will be avenged, the past of
infamy will be avenged, pending accounts will be settled, the
mercenaries will be shot. There will be no mercenaries. No one
will any longer attempt to halt History. Only those who will thrust
it into the future will remain. Gaby read Fanon. His fury seemed
devastating to her. All the more so because it was black. All the
more so because it was cultured. How could he help but hate the
white colonizer with all his guts? He speaks of *absolute violence.*
Is, she asks herself, killing Aramburu absolute violence? "The col-
onized is ready at any moment for violence." But Fanon advances
towards fearful limits. Even she, who fears no one, at times
wavers. The word *madness* makes her dizzy. It is not a humanistic
dizziness—something that would make her say to herself, "How
am I going to kill someone like me, another human being?" That
is humanitarian shit. Gandhian tripe. If someone kills someone

else it is because that other is not, for him, someone in his own likeness. Not another human being. Aramburu the gunman is not my likeness nor "another" human being. He is only an assassin. An assassin in the service of the regime of exploitation. That strips him of his humanity. Humanity wins. It wins by being on the side of the cause of mankind. The cause of mankind is liberty. The death of oppression. The liberation of the country. The creation of a new humanity. Of a new man. Anyone opposed to this lacks humanity. What will keep us from killing him? Fanon, in the face of the colonizer, rejects any method that is not violent. For the oppressed, *only this madness,* violence, can pull them out of colonial oppression. Are we, then, mad? Yes, mad for justice. Mad because we are not sane. Sane men do not risk their lives. We do. We risk our lives for the liberation of others, of all of the oppressed of this earth. We are, then, mad with love. And don't try to tell me that's something a woman would say. It must be what any revolutionary would say. We kill for love.

Gaby does not stay with the others. She has other things to do—none of them less important than those of her comrades. They reach the intersection of Figueroa Alcorta and Pampa. Gaby—whom they call Skinny—Maza, and Monkey Vélez get out of the pickup. They're carrying the bags with the uniforms. They're carrying their guns. And they go to a friend's house. They have a decisive mission: to write something that will explode in the newsrooms of all the newspapers. Something the announcers will read over and over again, thousands of times, with a voice of alarm, full of pain and also a dark fear, indefinable: the fear of knowing that something terrible has just happened in the country.

Ramus and Capuano sit in the front of the pickup. Aramburu, Fernando, and Firmenich are in back. The young centurions are beginning to feel that things are going just fine. Even too well. Will it be that easy? Or is destiny preparing a surprise for them? They don't think very much. There is no time. A little bit later, another change. They climb into a Gladiator. None of this is very important. They have another goal: *Timote*. They know how to get there. They studied the route for one long month. A direct route. What does *direct* mean? That it avoids any police stops. It isn't out of fear that they choose this route. Any policeman who shows up will be a dead policeman. But it would be better to avoid that. Fernando now senses, deep down, the taste of triumph. Everything has been easy. Everything continues to be easy. Why deny it: it's easy to kill someone in Argentina. If it's easy with Aramburu, it's easy with anyone. The question surprises him: Will it be that way with them? They are the wind. They cannot be caught. They are nowhere and they are prepared to be everywhere. They are the urban guerrilla movement, and the urban guerrilla movement is invincible. No one can attack it. It's like sand. It slips through the hands of power. And it is like rock: when it strikes, it kills.

Of the three who are riding in back, let's talk about Firmenich. He is twenty-two years old. A Catholic and a nationalist, he graduated with a gold medal from the Colegio Nacional de Buenos Aires. He will not be the hero of the hour, although he will have a lot to say during the questioning of Aramburu. Good novels avoid describing the physical appearance of characters. Firmenich needs it less than many. You meet him. You don't like him much. Or you hate him. Or you question him. Or there are still those fanatics who get really upset if you fail to put him on the altar they want for him. An enigmatic person, it would be the same thing to say he was an authentic revolutionary as an agent of the CIA. There's still a lot of time left. But this man, who will first go on to take over the leadership of the Montoneros, will give the order, in a brutally mistaken act, for the assassination of a union man few would die for out of love, but one they certainly did not want to see dead. Perón, the first among them. Now he watches the countryside and feels proud. "This is a cakewalk," he says. And it is. In all his life as an operative, which is already extensive, he cannot remember an easier, more simple escape, with fewer obstacles than this one. And they really screwed Aramburu! He's worried a little bit about reaching the General Paz Highway. He knows it's full of cars and trucks. Sometimes quite a lot of them. Sometimes there are traffic backups. Often there are police to prevent them. Today there is no sign of either. They exit at Gaona and follow dirt roads they know, ones they studied beforehand. There'll be no problems. If you plan things well, operations don't go wrong. This one will not go wrong, the one they've named Operation Pindapoy, after the name of an orange juice. Hard to know for what other reason.

They have to cross the Luján River. They know how to do it.

There's an old, solid bridge, well built. They tried it. It's wooden, but it will hold them. They take eight hours to go a distance that should take four. But they avoid anyplace where danger might be lurking. Because that's how it is: you can't see the dangers. They hide and then surprise us. Today, one surprised Aramburu, in that now he's with them and not in his house with his wife, drinking that coffee that he would surely drink after lunch, before conspiring on how to give life to the regime, to create a Peronismo in a "shirt and tie." No, General. Today you had a problem. But not an unexpected one. Maybe you consider it unexpected. But that problem dates back many years. When you signed Decree no. 4161. Or the day Valle was executed. Or when Eva disappeared. You did everything possible to be where you are now. Your destiny, being brought to justice, was designed by you alone. From that point of view, *we are your creation.* Or not just yours. We are the perfect, impeccable creation of right-wing Argentina. What else did you expect to engender? Obedient youngsters who would accept submissively your arbitrary, disdainful actions? There are no youngsters like that. A man is young when he knows how to align himself with injustice. And you brought the natural injustice to any people subjugated to capitalistic exploitation and political abandonment, depriving the people of their leader and banning them from saying the name of their beloved leader, about whom not only do they recall happy, sunny times, in which they felt themselves to be an essential part of the country and not its castoffs, its poorly paid laborers, those who are offended and insulted for their hard work. And you deprived them of their standard-bearer: Eva, the woman who loved them to the point of consuming herself in the fire of that love, so ardent was she.

Now they, through us, seek their revenge. If those who have been humiliated do not rebel, there will always be youngsters pure of heart who will do it for them, showing the way, taking up the vanguard. Go fuck yourself, General. The time to settle accounts has arrived.

Let us turn our attention to Aramburu. Can we presume to know what he thinks? Is it possible? He sits there in silence. What does a man who knows himself surrounded by his enemies think about, a man accompanied by his kidnappers, who do not speak to him either? At times silence in that Gladiator pickup must have turned into shouting. Is he afraid they are going to kill him? Can he accept the possibility that they would dare to take him out? No, they'll converse with him. They'll let him know what they want. Kidnapping him is kidnapping a man who converses with the highest power in the republic. Maybe even he might be that power. Those kidnapping him are making themselves heard and who, if he listened to them, might heed some or all of his petitions. Today he will concede quite a few. He is prepared to say yes. To promise. Then he'll see later. But if it's a matter of telling them that he will do what they want, then he will. They are very young. Everyone young is an idealist. As they say, an incendiary at twenty, a fireman at forty. He will be expansive, generous, even hearty. Yes, he's going to get out of this. We believe that Aramburu must have thought something like that on the long trip on potted, dusty, muddy roads.

Let us suppose we decide to say something about the place where they are going. It is not a harebrained decision. What is going to happen is going to happen there. Rather than being harebrained, it is logical to say something about the place. If one were to write a novel that takes place in Tartagal, it must say something about Tartagal. If it takes place in Niza, about Niza. Somewhat less, because almost everyone knows something about Niza. Or they've seen it in the movies. Not to mention Paris. It would be immoral to describe Rome. But the Gladiator pickup is on its way to Timote. Sarmiento said about his *Facundo,* "I invented anecdotes in accord." He said it with pride, defiantly. We also must invent our own. We have already done so. No one should be bothered by that. If what we've invented is verisimilar, it's welcome. Someone could ask this: How do you know that Aramburu said that? Or Abal Medina? We don't know. We weren't there with a tape recorder. Others will say the body took three bullets, not four. Or that it wasn't a Peugeot 404, but a 505. Too many things are sought with respect to Aramburu. The principal one is that Onganía ordered him killed by Imaz, his Minister of the Interior. Firmenich was his accomplice. A double agent. He visited the Ministry of the Interior more than twenty times before May 29. These are theories without any significant basis. The one that most fits is the one we choose. The Onganía-Imaz-Montoneros thesis includes a person who undermines it: Captain Gandhi. A madman from the overthrow of Perón who had Juan Duarte's head cut off. He showed it to Cámpora. "Tell me the truth, Dr. Cámpora. Did he commit suicide or did you people commit it for him?" Meanwhile, the head lies on the desk. There's a large hole in it. Gandhi inserts a pencil in it and rotates it: "It's a large hole for a .38." Juancito Duarte had left behind a charming suicide note in which he said he blew his brains out with a .38. And then he added, "Please excuse the handwriting. Please forgive me for everything." The animal Captain Gandhi (Captain González Alvariño, another gem of the overthrow, macabre and possessed by necrophilia) insists on showing the head to Cámpora: "Look at this hole. That's not from a .38. It's from a .45. He didn't commit suicide. You people killed him." Just to prove that the Peronistas were assassins. Especially Perón. He had even ordered the death of Evita's brother. It's this guy, with his reality base, they turn to prove the thesis of the Onganía-Imaz-Montonero alliance. Poppycock. Onganía leaves the government a few days later. Imaz as well. What use is Aramburu's death to them? So they would be fired as incompetents. No, sir: Aramburu's death is the spectacular appearance of the true Peronista guerrilla movement. Everything before had been nothing by comparison to this. Even less so the Tacuara Nationalist Movement, the Tacuara Revolutionary Nationalist Movement, and the Nationalist Restoration Guard these kids had come out of. The other guerrilla organizations are unable to understand them. What is the meaning of "May God, Our Lord, take pity on his soul"? That had nothing to do with Marx, or Lenin, or Castro, nor with Che or Mao or

any-fucking-body else, excuse my French. If you rub someone
out, who doesn't ask for something from God? Not even that He
"take pity on his soul." Especially for Him to "take pity on his
soul." But if you rub someone out, you begin to get all fucked up
with "Thou shalt not kill." And if you're Catholic enough to think
about the soul of the guy you're rubbing out, don't rub him out,
brother. Set aside those Sunday ceremonies of priest, hosts, bless-
ings. Forget all that fervor of a brand-new altar boy. But that's how
the Montoneros were. That surprising phrase "May God have pity
on your soul" said a lot. First, that they believed in God. And God
is a reactionary. Everybody knows that. Second, they believed in
divine mercy in a twentieth century that, if it had demonstrated
anything, it had shown its human evil, a limitless evil. An absent
God. A God who, if he had any idea of what was going on, was a
son of a bitch. He was evil, not good. Because he stopped nothing. Even theologians said it: "After Auschwitz it is impossible to
imagine a totally good God." Third, they believed in the soul! That
took the cake. They were hopeless: the non-Catholic sectors close
to Peronismo couldn't swallow that. They said that that's fascism.
Peronismo plus God plus pity plus soul plus guns plus individualist, anarchic shock troops equals Catholic fascism. You've got to
watch out for those types. For everything that wasn't part of the
Montoneros, Peronismo was something else: the politics of the
masses. The fronts of the masses. Student mobilizations. And the
great theoreticians. Not God. Marxism and Hegel and Sartre and
Algeria. Including the "national question," of course.

   Timote is far removed from these passions. Everything History
brushes becomes important. We wouldn't give three cents for
Timote. Timote, without Aramburu's death, is worthless, nonex-

istent. Timote, with Aramburu's death, becomes part of History.
A human project made it theirs. If peas grew in Iraq, no one
would speak of Iraq. But let petroleum gush forth and—because
it gushes forth—blood does, too. A human project included Iraq
in its urgencies. The empire needs petroleum. It can't stop the
machinery of armaments. Iraq, thus, becomes virtually the center
of the universe. In 1970, which is where we are, the Montoneros
decide to try Aramburu in Timote. And then they kill him and
bury him there. From that tragedy on, Timote becomes a part of
history. That tiny town in the Province of Buenos Aires, located
in the parish of Carlos Tejedor, founded in 1876 by General Con-
rado Villegas, who wanted to pay homage to Lieutenant Colonel Don Pedro Timote, a military man who had distinguished
himself in the struggles against the Indians, in the border wars,
in the slaughter that the armies of civilization carried out with
precision, leaving not a soul alive, against the savages who were
a bother to the life of men of goodwill, men of the land, who
created a solid, protective fort. That small village that still has,
in the twenty-first century, barely 509 inhabitants, whose postal
code is B6457, which had a bar named El Moderno (and maybe
still does—is it important?), a movie house and, only a few blocks
away, another movie house that competed with it, and which
had a hotel and a church. That small village that fools who spent
their infancy there yearn after, does not exist nor did it ever exist.
It is now about to exist. Because there is a Gladiator pickup that
covers the 420 kilometers that separates it from the capital. History is a passenger in that pickup. No sooner will it enter Timote
than the village will cease forever to be what it was. Someone of
those who still today agree to talk about the settlement lament

that it has come to be something, a signifier. "See, what bothers me," says one of the inhabitants who still dresses like a gaucho, like the prolongation of a heroic defeat, that of the nineteenth century of which he is only a leftover, a wreck who does not even know he is because he doesn't even know, in a remote time, that the gauchos fought to defend their dignity, which he has long ago tamely forfeited to his bosses. "See, what bothers me," as we said he was saying, "is that in this quiet town, with its noble people, in this town where people work, a crime as horrendous as the killing of Aramburu has been committed, because that sullied Timote, understand. It makes me ashamed people come here and only ask about that. Like you, mister. Excuse my directness."

"And what would you like them to ask about?" we say to him.

He acts a bit annoyed. He says, "You don't think there's anything else to ask about? Look around you. Look at the plaza. Listen to the birds chirping. Listen to the church bell at midday. Eat something. Some ribs. Follow it with some good wine. Take a nice nap. Those things are life. Aramburu, that's death."

"Maybe. But, tell me this: What do you want me to ask you about the chirping of the birds and the church bell? Pardon me, but I'm going to be frank with you: I wouldn't even spend two days here. If Timote exists, if it's worth the trouble to come this far and if there's something to ask about it's Aramburu, friend. And the Montoneros that brought him, tried him and killed him. One comes to Timote for the blood."

He sucks for a long time on the straw of his *mate*. "Go to the city," he says. "Go live with problems, all nervous and screwed up. And die, young man. That's the law of the urban jungle."

We shake hands with him and thank him for the chat and the

information. We avoid telling him that, for us, he's already dead. Why torture him? Let him have death throes without realizing it. Let him go on living, unaware that he lived like a clam, like an amoeba. We say this because we believe that there are not monumentous events in the life of an amoeba.

We depart Timote just as we came. With nothing. Nothing comes from nothing. Why did we go? We knew that there were no traces left there. It was like a task we had to complete. If we have given ourselves the task of writing about the crime in Timote, let's travel to Timote. Now we can say it. Just this: we were there. We were only able to see one unexpected thing: the place where, a month after the Aramburu event, they found Don Blas Acébal, the foreman, dead. He was lying in the brush, smelling bad and full of stab wounds. Strange, isn't it? The police were not interested in the matter. Just one more servant stabbed to death. Another peon who died a bad death, no matter if he was the foreman. The guy wouldn't have seen a thing. Probably something to do with women, a gambling debt, a drunken brawl. Nothing. Too bad. We liked Don Blas Acébal. Or we like the sort of person we made him into. If that's who he was then not even God, that friend of the Montoneros, could know. And it really doesn't matter to us. But we'll take a chance: we would swear that the Acébal who will appear in this story cannot have been much different from the real one, the one who unfortunately ended up in the brush, stabbed to death, smelling foul. What you call a man with a sad end. Nevertheless, a month before that bad end, life had provided him with the happiest lay of his life. We will get to see him in that joyful trance.

They arrive at La Celma around 5:30 or 6:00 in the evening. It's a ranch house. It's not foreign to them. They do not enter a place that doesn't belong to them. It belongs to Carlos Gustavo Ramus's family. Aramburu realizes this. That calms him down a bit. They are kids from good families, families linked to the land, to the country. They get out. They walk toward the house. Suddenly, a problem. Every ranch has a loyal foreman. He's the type of man who devotes his life to a family, to taking care of their property, living in close quarters with the owners without ever, ever thinking he's part of them. The foreman has to be a man without ambitions, a simple soul, an obedient soul, someone who finds his happiness in the happiness of the owners. The man is Basque and his name is Acébal, about whom we already know a few things. Ramus goes to meet him. He does not want the loyal servant to approach the revolutionary group. Ramus knows how to talk to him. Every owner knows how to talk to his foreman. He knows how to share his *mate*. Eat his crackers. Ask after his wife, whose name he will know. And after his kids, whose names he will also know. Then, as always, he will press a generous amount of money into his rough hands, punished by decades of labor. And he will call him "Don." And he will say to him, "Hey, fellow, what's up?" That "fellow" is important. It's a tie. An intimate gesture. The owner comes down to the world of the foreman. If he

doesn't know how to do it, he's not a good owner. He also knows
how to take his leave. He knows how to leave the foreman alone,
in his world. And he will join his own. Worlds that do not, nor
will they ever, touch. But that is no denial of what is constructed
in that moment they share, which belongs to both of them: "How
are things going, Don Acébal?"

"Great, Carlos. Everything's in order. And with you?" Don
Acébal calls Ramus *Carlos* and even speaks to him familiarly.
He has known him since he was a child. From when he would
run around the place, sometimes getting in the way, making a
bunch of noise. From when he learned how to ride. From when
he became a teenager and began to show up with some girl-
friends. But Don Acébal had always been the same: a grown man
getting along in years, the foreman—the one who takes care of
everything, the one who looks, the one who stands watch when
the owners leave. That's why Carlos always speaks to him with
respect. This would only surprise people from the city. Everything
is clear in the countryside: if the foreman has known the owner's
son since he was a puppy, the owner's son will never cease to be
what he is—the owner's son, the landowner. But the foreman is
the man who saw him grow up. A powerful figure, strong. Besides, Acébal is himself quite a character.

Ramus tells him to go take a stroll. Perhaps he can go to town
that night. That's why he gives him a good amount of money,
more than usual. Not too much: he doesn't want Acébal to get
suspicious. But just the right amount. "Go have a good time, Don
Acébal. Tomorrow's another day. And if you want to take it off,
too, be my guest. I don't need you right now. One or two days, no
more. If I need something, I'll go into town to find you. Stay the
night at Riganti's Grocery Store. He's your friend, right?"

"One of the few I have left."

"And the others? Have you had a fight with everyone?"

Don Acébal sadly shakes his head, clicks his tongue and slowly says, "You can sure tell you're young, Carlos. At my age you don't lose friends over disagreements or gambling and less over women. You lose them because they die off."

"No shit, Acébal. You've got a way to go before the Reaper comes for you. By the way . . ." Even though it wasn't part of his plans, he gives him a few more pesos. "Take advantage of the fact you're still a bull. I bet you've got a hot chick in town. Don't deny yourself."

Don Acébal turns red. It's the first time the owner has said something like that to him. "But not today, Don Carlos. Nor tomorrow. Your parents don't like it."

"When, then?"

"Only on Sunday, which is my day off."

"I told you, Don Acébal, I'm giving you the day off. It's Sunday until I call you or go looking for you. Besides, what kind of crap did my parents say to you? Sunday is the Lord's Day, not the day for sinning."

"Look, Don Carlos, I'm going to tell you something. I'm telling you because I know you're our friend. You were from the time you were little. As far as the owners are concerned, between being a slacker with God and being a slacker with work, they prefer you to be a slacker with God."

Ramus laughs out loud and pats Acébal affectionately on the shoulder and says, "Take the buggy, tell Don Riganti to give you a room, and have a good time."

"Thanks, Don Carlos. You always were a good boy. I've known

you since . . . Look, I even taught you how to gallop like the Indians."

"We never went on a raid."

"There are no more raids. Even the gauchos are all gone, Don Carlos."

"Where'd you get that, Acébal?" Ramus says and feels good that what he's going to say to him is more for himself, because there's no way Acébal is going to be suspicious of what he's saying, because not even he fully believes it himself, although it's growing on him. This is what he says: "You never know when some are going to show up."

"I can take the buggy, then?"

"Of course. And a word of advice, Acébal. Forget the Reaper or you won't have a good time even with the hottest chick in town."

"If I can, OK. But I don't know. Something tells me he's not too far away."

They say good-bye. Ramus watches him walk away. He thinks, *There's nothing you can do with these country types. They don't miss a thing.* He barely had any contact with Aramburu; he didn't see him, nor does he know he's here. He hasn't got the foggiest idea of what we're going to do, and he can already smell the Reaper.

Anybody would understand and accept the fact that Ramus can't say a word to his foreman about what's happening. However, there's an undeniable fact that requires our attention: the only person from the village that appears throughout the whole story is completely sidelined, the one most distanced from the limelight. There's a certain paradox lurking in this complete whole.

Aramburu is not wearing his jacket. He's also not wearing
a tie. He still doesn't have a clear picture of what's happening.
This will not last long: perhaps soon everything will be all too
clear. They put him in one of the bedrooms. The youngsters go
about without talking. Possibly they smoke. People smoked a lot
then. We don't know if Aramburu has asked for a cigarette. We
don't know if they offer him one. At least a cup of coffee? They
owe him at least this much consideration. He, or his wife, offered them a cup of coffee. But the young people seem focused
on what they are about to put in motion. Nothing less than the
trial. These youngsters, twenty-two or twenty-three years old, are
going to try a sixty-seven-year-old veteran general. Someone who
is almost an old man. Let's keep the date in mind: 1970. A lot of
years have gone by. In 1970, and especially for kids twenty-two or
twenty-three years old, someone sixty-seven years old was an old
man, or at least decidedly a senior. But Fernando and Firmenich
do not see it that way. They see him as one of the country's historical landmarks, a heartless protagonist. Although this verdict
may still be awaiting the appropriate trial. If it needs to be. Is
it necessary to pass judgment on someone you've kidnapped
because you think he's guilty of unforgivable crimes, ones that
are irreversible and unworthy of clemency? It's possible that the

kidnappers themselves sincerely ponder this question among themselves.

There is another bed facing Aramburu's. Fernando sits down on it. He rests his elbows on his thighs and knits his hands together. He stares at the General. He says to him, "General, we are a revolutionary Peronista organization. We picked you up because we are going to subject you to a revolutionary trial."

Now Aramburu understands everything. He understands it and accepts it without effort. Let's ask ourselves here, Was he expecting this? He knew that Peronista guerrilla groups were in existence. They did things now and then, nothing serious. Did he ever believe they would bother him? If he did, nothing shows that he was bothered. He says, "All right."

The conversation between Ramus and Acébal would not
have lasted more than half an hour. Ramus entered the house in
search of his companions. Don Acébal put on his Sunday clothes
and packed a small bag of clothes. Something told him that the
best thing he could do was to put a fair, healthy distance between
himself and the ranch. A good stretch, a distance that would lift a
weight from his soul. The owner had told him: disappear, Acébal.
He had even told him to go find a woman. Nothing like that had
ever happened before. If something like that was happening now
it was because something not right was about to take place. Besides, he had no idea when Don Carlos's parents would be back.
They were probably off somewhere in Europe. They often went
for two, three months at a time. Then they'd return all smiles,
heavier, tanned, and laden down with gifts for the help. Acébal
was not stupid: he knew they got them cheap. And if something
made them valuable it was that they came from Europe or the
United States. As far as he was concerned, another world. Places
he'd never go. The owners went and came back with baubles.
Smiling, submissive, faithful almost to the point of losing his
dignity—but not too much so—he would accept the colored bits
of glass. He had taken good care of the ranch. Everything is in
order, boss. Everything is just like it was before you left. As soon

as you want, leave again. He had his back covered. Don Acébal, who was infallible, had it covered for him. But not this time. Something was afoot. Carlitos had crossed over the line. Was it a suspicion or a certainty? Damn, it was hard to know. On other occasions, he and those who came with him would bring some attractive girls along. They would play music, dance, and then— just as nature ordered for animals and people—some would go off in pairs, because it's not healthy to hold back when you get the hots. And those kids were youngsters. And the girls were, too—and someone had told him that the ones from good families, the rich girls, the upper-class girls usually were no convent nuns, but rather whores, all-out sluts. Either it was true or it was the bad-mouthing of the poor. People who said nasty things because they were envious. Because there wasn't one of them, in their whole fucking lives, who would ever get off with one of these jewels. Including him. But he was resigned. He didn't need TV beauties or Rambler or Ford or Wilson cologne models (the model for the latter really made him all hot and bothered, almost beyond control), nor the women for Uvita wine (*Uvita, ta, ta, ta, ta, drink Uvita wine and then tell me how it went, ta, ta, ta ta*), nor the celebrity Claudia Sánchez (he did know who she was), nor even that hunk of a woman sprawled on the tiger rug, the one who did the Carlos Gardel rum commercial, the one whose name the guys in the grocery store in the know told him—a name that, truth be told, meant little or nothing to him, because this woman was as inaccessible to him as the Queen of England or Elizabeth Taylor who, no matter how far along in years she was, still gave him the hots, an unfathomable burning, like that powerful dame, the one in the Carlos Gardel rum ad, who, in a cavern-

ous voice, says to this guy, "Give it to me, Carlos," and the guy
reaches up for the bottle and gives it to her and the announcer
says, "Carlos Gardel rum, like no other," and that jerk Onganía
banned it because someone told the dumb army idiot that "give
it to me" and "fuck me" were the same thing, that they were
used interchangeably—or Zulma Faiad in that somewhat earlier
ad in which Zulma, covered with a piece of lettuce, dances half
naked and a guy disguised as a tomato says to another disguised
as a cucumber, "That lettuce's got it all." The main point for Don
Acébal was this, what the piece of lettuce had was a full salad,
and that the dusky women of the village, the gaucho women or
those little Indian girls who were not even fourteen years old and
who liked to fuck their brains out, would put out for him without
any problem. So he had no reason to complain. To each his own.
The question is whether you like what you can get. There is no
other secret for happiness in this friggin' life fraught with danger,
sinkholes no one gets out of alive. That's what everyone's after:
happiness. That's what no one finds. It's as easy as that. You learn
to live with what you get. And it doesn't take long after you've resigned yourself to liking it. And if you really resign yourself, you'll
like it forever. It's the others he doesn't like. They're really skinny
and, so he's been told, spend their time flitting from one party to
another. You've got to have very expensive cars to pick those ones
up and take them to hotels that are also very expensive. Their
legs are too long. Their teeth are too large and too white, blind-
ingly so. They must smell of perfumes from foreign countries.
Our dusky women smell like mares, of sweat, they've got hair in
their armpits—as they should, as is natural, because if it weren't,
it wouldn't grow there—and they smell of sex, damn it; that's

the best part, what most sets a man off, makes him hot, he sees them coming and from half a block away he can smell the damp fragrance of their demanding, hungry cunts that won't settle for just anything. Fuck it, no! They won't buy the stuff about it being short but thick. Or skinny but long. Or skinny and short, but rearing to go. You blew it, brother. They want a cock that is long, thick, and ready to go. And if it isn't, forget it, try as hard as you can, use your tongue all you want like José María Muñoz and Antonio Carrizo and even Mareco, going at it together, because satisfied, like really satisfied, they're hard to please, it's as easy as that. What women, what mares we've got here and don't come bothering me with the skinny kind they've got in Buenos Aires, who don't even look like they're Argentine, they look like dames from any part of the world. You fuck one and it's like fucking them all or no one. Afterward you're not even sure where you stuck it. That's what the friend of Carlos Ramus's father had said one afternoon there in La Celma—Cacho Rivarola, who had roamed the world in search of a new hole, something that would surprise him. And nothing. "Nothing, Don Acébal. They all smell the same, fuck the same, there's not one different from all the rest." He stared at him hard. Something fundamental was about to be said. Cacho Rivarola said, "Don Acébal, do me a favor. I'm begging you on my knees. Get one of those dark women for me, anyone of your servants. Fat, big boobs, dirty, maybe slutty. Tell me where she is and I'll go there. It's my last hope." And that was Cacho Rivarola, one of Argentina's last playboys.

Don Acébal pulls the buggy up at the village grocery store. It's 9:15 PM. He had polished the buggy. He wanted it to look nice. That evening he feels free, almost wealthy. The grocery store is called "The Painkiller." The owner is neither a gaucho or an Argentine. He's Italian. He came to the country as a little kid. And he worked and set himself up finally in Timote. Nothing to speak of. But the fate of a working man. A good man. Because he has some property and hopes to buy more. His name is Franco Riganti. And Don Acébal has just arrived with a purpose: to make a surprising revelation to him. Don Franco's going to drop dead when he tells him, Don Acébal thinks with a secret, sweet pleasure. He parks the buggy and walks toward the door of the grocery store.

He looks calm to the youngsters. If he's faking it, he does it
very well. Fernando attempts to take some photographs of him,
but the camera acts up. They use a tape recorder for the trial.
Hoping they won't have the same luck. The tape recorder fulfills
its function: it records the entire trial. They must have used a lot
of tapes because the trial drags on much longer than they had
planned. The youngsters don't want to pressure him, they don't
want, as Firmenich will say many years later, to intimidate him.
As in so many other things, we don't believe him. Aramburu the
Basque man does not seem to be a man who would be intimidat-
ed. He notes how the youngsters drag out their questions. There
are a few strategic pauses to give him enough time to answer with
precision. He takes advantage of them. He doesn't know why, but
he believes that every delay works in his favor. Aramburu is slow
to answer, looks for time, trying to make the interrogation stretch
on endlessly. He knows that half the country must be looking for
him. The more time he gains, the more time they have to find
him. He answers in vagaries.

"I don't know," he says. Or "I don't remember." He supposes
that the failure of memory can save him. If he remembers nothing, what can they accuse him of? What can these kids know?
What they read. What they were told. But what proof do they

have? In the absence of proof, they depend on his confession. Let us suppose that he refuses to answer. What will they do? He doesn't like that option.

Fernando paces around the room again. Finally, he says, "I'm going to state the first major charge against you. You, General, in June 1956, ordered the execution of General Valle and other patriots who were part of the same uprising."

Aramburu answers immediately. One can tell that he has worked out this answer over the years. It's not the first time they've mentioned this unpleasant incident to him and it's not the first time that he gives an answer that satisfies him. One he believes covers and protects him. Makes him innocent. "That's not the way it was," he says. "I wasn't in Buenos Aires when those lamentable events occurred."

"Lamentable?"

"Lamentable. It was all lamentable. The ridiculous attempted coup and the executions. I was in Rosario. I couldn't stop them."

"That's not true, General," Fernando says. "We have proof."

The proof is implacable. It has often been said that we are what we do. If that's the case, no one escapes their past. But I am not what I was. I've changed. I no longer hate the Peronistas; I want to make them a part of democracy. I would no longer execute anyone. I believe that's now a part of the past, or at least that's where it should be. You can't build a country on the basis of hate. Why do these youngsters make me remember Valle? I'm not the same person who had Valle executed. The years have not gone by for me in vain. I'm sixty-seven. I haven't lived in vain. I've lived to change. To overcome my mistakes. My judges are too young to understand that. They think you don't change. They think you're always the same person you were when you were young. They think that way because they're proud to be what they are and don't want to change. But you can change into something better than what you were. They would never understand. They felt, today, that they will never be better than they are now, at this moment. They will never be any more pure or idealistic than they are now. It would be difficult to convince them otherwise. A dispirited Aramburu knows that: these youngsters have frozen him in June 1956. They are trying *that* Aramburu. By doing so, they believe that the one before them today is also that one. For the avenger, his victim must *always* be the same person who committed the act that demands revenge.

All vengeance requires the abolition of time. If the avenger were to concede to his victim the benevolence of the time that has transpired, everything would have to be reformulated. There's no one who doesn't change with time. We've established that fact. It's part of common sense. We all change. We all cease to be, at least, *exactly* who we were at some other time. Our victim is no longer the one who committed the act for which we judged him. Yet it doesn't matter. What his victim has become is not important to the avenger. Maybe today he is the purest of the archangels. If the time that has gone by since the act for which he is condemned has changed him, or the temporal space in which he did it, that time ends up annulled. The avenger, obsessively, concentrates on a single moment in the life of his victim. A single moment, a single act. He doesn't budge from that. If what provokes revenge are various acts and not only one, there will then be other moments. But each act for which the victim is condemned will remain irremediably tied to the moment it happened. Nothing he has done since will change a thing. *You, whom we now propose to try, have been and will always be for all eternity the man who has committed the act or the acts for which he is now in the uncomfortable position of the accused. Those individuals who are usually killed for the things they did in a past that is an eternal present. Which is today. Because we have annulled, abolished the time in which you could have become someone else. You, for us, will never be someone else.*

"Especially Decree no. 10364, General," Fernando says. "That's the one that orders, by direct decision of the executive power, which means *you*, that those responsible for the uprising be executed. How could you tell Valle's wife you were sleeping? No one who can sign a decree like that can sleep."

"My conscience is clean," Aramburu says. "I was certain of my acts. Listen, we made a revolution. We did it against a government that was antidemocratic, tyrannical, which fed class hatred. A revolution requires determination in order to survive. There were a lot of Peronistas and they conspired incessantly. Finally, Valle undertook a counterrevolution against us. We squashed it. And we lined the counterrevolutionaries up in front of a firing squad. I trust I don't have to give you lessons on this: every revolution executes the counterrevolutionaries."

Does Aramburu realize what he has just said? Has he just signed his own death warrant? What idea does he think the youngsters who are trying him feel about themselves? They told him, "We are a revolutionary organization." What does he think he is for these revolutionaries? A counterrevolutionary. If every revolution has the right to execute the counterrevolutionaries, what does he expect those who are trying him to do? No one, in the midst of this tense climate, recalls a sentence they all know—Aramburu because he read it as an admirer of Lavalle. His young captors because they read it as fanatics of Dorrego, whom, in some way, they are also avenging today. It is the sentence from Salvador María del Carril, that cold centralist who sought to convince Lavalle to kill Dorrego. It went more or less like this: "A revolution is a gamble in which you win even the lives of the vanquished."

"We want to read you some declarations by Admiral Rojas," Firmenich says.

"Why me and not him?" Aramburu says brusquely. "If there is a right-wing thug in this country it's Rojas. He also decided the executions. And many other things. If it had been up to him . . ." He stops. He thinks better of it. He says, "Of the two, I'm the moderate. He . . ."

"He's the clown," Fernando interrupts him. "He's the animal. You were always the intelligent one. The one who decided things. And you're the one who is now mixed up in something that is possibly the main motive for this trial?"

"Which is?"

"You'll find out. I return to Rojas's declarations. He accused Valle and his accomplices of being Marxists and amoral."

"You see? I would never have done that. How could I say such a thing? How could I say that about Valle? A Catholic, a family man . . ."

"We need for you to sign a declaration. Saying what you have just told us—that Valle was neither a Marxist nor immoral. That Rojas lied."

As though surprised, Aramburu leans back and spreads his hands.

"That's what you want?"

"Yes."

"But that . . . we could have done that in my house."

Fernando Abal barely smiles. It's the first time he does so.

"You're not following me, General. We want this and other things as well. We want you to tell us about the coup against Onganía. You're the leader and the goal is to bring Peronismo into the system. Dress it up in a tie and jacket. Tame it. Turn it over to the liberal democratic regime of the ruling classes."

"I don't interpret it that way. But I can understand you might."
Aramburu stops. Doesn't he want to go on talking? He furrows
his brow. He purses his lips as though to prevent the words from
escaping. Finally, he says, "If you want to talk about that, turn the
tape recorder off. It's too important."

"But it's not what's *most* important," Fernando says.

"We want to talk about something much more important,
General," Firmenich says. "Much more important."

Aramburu falls into one of his long silences. But he's not
staring off into space. It's evident he's thinking. He's not trying to
avoid it. But why take so long? Is it because he's careful, sensible,
he likes to choose his words, find the right expression? Or is it
simply that he's slow? Our guess is the opposite; we said it: he
needs time. He needs to gain time for those who are looking for
him.

All he asks is, "What?"

Fernando is somewhat removed. He's standing. He looks
down on him. He dryly says, "We want to talk about Evita Perón's
body."

Aramburu was waiting for that. He was afraid of it. Since they
took so long to mention it, he thought it wasn't at issue. But here
it is: Eva Perón. There's no such thing as a Peronista who doesn't
get furious at the mention of the name of that woman they have
had so vilely whisked away from them. There is no revenge Eva
Perón does not justify, does not cry out for. There is no way to
repair that insult.

Aramburu knows now that he is in danger.

Let us suppose that Aramburu says, "There's not much I can tell you about Eva Perón's body."

Let us suppose that Firmenich says, "This is not the time to talk about that."

Fernando approaches him. He likes to stare at Aramburu. Especially when he says important things to him. Like now.

"You're planning an overthrow of the state. If you deny it, we won't believe you. We have good sources."

"Like what?"

Fernando names a pair of generals.

"You confuse friends with conspirators," Aramburu says.

With a swift gesture, Fernando turns the tape recorder off. It's a Geloso that's quite a few years old, but offers the security of well-made things. He says, "Now you can speak at ease."

Aramburu does not speak other than to say, "I'm hungry."

They put a quick light lunch together. No wine. Only soft drinks. Or water. When he sets a bottle of Coca-Cola on the table, Firmenich, who smiles more than Fernando, says, "Imperialism's best invention."

Let us suppose that Ramus, who comes in and out, serving as a contact with exterior reality, says with irony, "As far as the General is concerned, imperialism's best invention is imperialism."

"You're wrong about me," Aramburu says. "I'm not an agent of imperialism. Onganía is. I'm a democrat."

"Don't play us for fools," Fernando says. "A democrat does not execute a comrade in arms in the National Penitentiary. Like a common criminal. Like a dog."

"You're also wrong there. That was in 1956. I wasn't a democrat. I was presiding over a revolutionary government. We had overthrown a dictator and we had to deal harshly with those who wanted to bring him back." Aramburu pauses. He looks at each of them one by one. "Now I'm a democrat. I'm a general who wants a broad, democratic government for his country. Broad— am I making myself clear? Including Peronismo. That's why I have to overthrow that animal Onganía. In order to accomplish that, I don't deny it, I have to conspire with the generals who named him, all men of goodwill, democrats like me."

"Right-wing thugs like you," Ramus says, somewhat imprudently.

"I'm not a right-wing thug. The right-wing thugs hate me. I'm the least thuggish of the men in the military. Listen, Onganía is on the way out. His time is up. That business in Córdoba sank him. It's only a matter of giving him a shove."

Franco Riganti has set a bottle of Bols on the table. That
warms up every get-together. Even more so if it's among friends.
Gin is a great thing. You've got to take it slowly. That's why you
drink it in those thick glasses that make so much noise when
you slam them down on the table. There's nothing more perfect
than gin—served in one of those small but solid glasses you can't
break with a stick—to make a point, sum things up categorically,
close a deal, emphasize a cuss word, make everyone know you're
leaving and leaving pissed off, you're not coming back, they
shouldn't wait for you, and maybe you'll never come back, damn
it. And as soon as you say damn it, you slam the glass on the table
and the glass makes a definitive noise, like a gong, and you get
up, adjust the knife in your belt, and walk out. You can only do
that God's way with a glass of gin. But there are two things you
must do. You not only slam the glass on the table, as though you
wanted to break it in two. First, you've got to down what's in the
glass. The gin. Here's how you do it: let's suppose you've had an
argument with someone. That you argued too much with him.
That you're fed up. You don't want to continue. You grab the glass
then. You say, "Look, pal." You lean your head back, open your
mouth, down the gin, swallow it, the glass is empty, you raise
your head, fix your gaze on your adversary, slam the glass on the
table, just as was said, as though you were trying to smash it, and

finish with, "Go fuck yourself." You get up and leave. The other guy stays glued to his chair. He doesn't move. Half stunned and half fucked over, his face has become as pale as a corpse's on the night of his wake, which is when everyone wants to eat sandwiches, tell jokes, down a few glasses of wine and get on their way as soon as possible because the dead, even those who are your friends—even them more than anyone else—inspire fear. And you've got to get to the corner grocery store, sit down at a table and ask Franco Rignati for a good glass of gin to get rid of the cold death has clamped in your guts which you can't easily get rid of, unless you really tie one on, and only then if you're lucky.

If we have indulged ourselves in the narrative style of the Buenos Aires gauchos, I'm sure you'll excuse us. It's just that Franco Riganti, who has already set that bottle of gin on the table, is talking to Don Acébal, because they're friends and are going to chat for a while. Acébal rather clumsily downs quite a few glasses.

"Take it easy, Blas," Riganti says to him. "Your hands are trembling. What the hell's going on?"

Acébal tries to calm down. The place is almost empty. And it's Friday at that. But the night is cold. Besides, the World Cup match against Peru starts on Sunday. Everyone's talking about that. People stay glued to the TV.

"If I tell you, you won't believe me," Acébal says.

Franco Riganti pours himself another gin. He says, "Whether I believe you or not, you'd better tell me. Because you can't go on that way. Spill the beans, fucker. Get it all out. It'll poison you otherwise."

"Did you see those kids from La Celma? Good kids."

"As far as I know, they are. Carlitos Ramus often comes around here. Always spends a bundle. He's a good client."

"Do you know who they brought to the ranch today?"

Riganti shakes his head. Acébal says, "Aramburu."

"You're messing with me. Keep your voice down."

"There's no one here."

"You've got to whisper things like that. Go on."

"Nothing else, Franco. They tried to distract me by keeping up a conversation. So I wouldn't see anything. Hell. I saw it all. It was Aramburu."

"You were smart to get out, Acébal. You have no idea of how the shit hits the fan in the country. Everyone says that Aramburu's been kidnapped. They're looking for him. They said right before sundown they were looking for him."

"That's a lie. Why the hell would they kidnap him? The General looked great . . ."

"Don't call that son of a bitch *General*. There's only one General."

"Crap. I always forget you're a Peronista. OK, let me finish. I just saw him from the corner of my eye, but I saw him. He was wearing just a shirt and seemed to be calm. As though he were going to have tea with the fellows."

Franco Riganti remains silent. He thinks for a long time. He furrows his brow so much that it makes a long and deep wrinkle, like a slit. At last he says, "You stay here, Acébal. You say you aren't a Peronista, but you're a man of the people. You've gone soft in the head from playing the role of the good little peon so long. But, as far as they're concerned, you're the enemy. The people."

"Who am I an enemy of?"

"Of them, Acébal. Of the Catholics and the military men. Tell me something."

He interrupts himself. The silence is like a thick bell jar, just like the gin glasses, isolating them from everything.

"Speak up," Acébal says.

"Those kids out at La Celma . . ."

"Yes."

"They're good Catholics, right?"

"Of course."

"Very, very good Catholics?"

"Yes, Franco. Just like their parents."

"Well, then, we're really fucked, old man."

"Why?"

"Look, Acébal, I don't want to ruin your night. But I can't hide the truth from you. Perón was overthrown by Aramburu. Along with the Church. The Catholics. They filled Government Square and screamed their lungs out: "Christ Has Won! Christ Has Won!" I can't forget it. The women in the kitchen, the poor people, and all the hands cried their eyes out. I got drunk and went to bed for two days. And now you tell me that, out there at La Celma, the Catholic jerks, just like in 1955, are meeting with that right-wing thug Aramburu."

Franco Riganti stands stock still, thinking. His gaze is lost in space. Acébal doesn't know what to say. He's sorry he brought him such a sad piece of news. Riganti shakes his head slowly, sorrowfully. Suddenly he says something. He says it in a whisper. So low that Acébal can hardly hear him.

Franco Riganti says, "It's a bad time for the Peronistas."

"Who's going to give it to him?" Fernando asks, who knows. "You?"

Aramburu is eating some uncured ham. There's also some good country cheese on his plate. He's drinking Coca-Cola. He doesn't answer Fernando's question. After all, they all know. The one who's going to give a shove to Onganía is him, no doubt about it. Him and all those who are with him. The problem is Gray-Head Lanusse, who'll not move a finger to save Onganía. But it's not likely he would get involved with a project in which he's not the protagonist. Lanusse is too big for his britches. For a good reason. It will be necessary to negotiate with him. Talk to him, give him some proposals. And if he wants the leadership, negotiate it with him. It's all negotiable except for two things. Peronismo must be legalized. And if it means bringing Perón back, then bring him back. "Even if it gives you an ulcer, Gray-Head. Even if it makes you sick. There's no other choice except to bring him back."

"The uncured ham is very good," he comments. "Real country style. These things are always ruined by the time they get to the city. It's the intermediaries. One of the disgraces of this country. They ruin the purity of products—either to make it easier to sell them or to increase their profits."

"Or both," Firmenich says.

"Or both," Aramburu agrees.

"But it's not the intermediaries," Fernando says. "It's capitalism. Capitalism is immoral."

"Getting back to Onganía," Aramburu says, ignoring Fernando's comment—which, of course, he does not agree with. "With Onganía overthrown, it's all very easy. A transition government."

"Another one?" Fernando says. Now he laughs sarcastically.

"Not just another one," Aramburu says. "The last one. If I preside over it, it's the last one. I give you my word. It will only last a few months. Just long enough to hold elections. With Peronismo part of the bargain. Do you understand? With Peronismo part of the mix. What you've been asking for since 1955."

"Part of what mix, General?" Fernando says.

Aramburu sets down his silverware. Surprised, he fixes his gaze on Fernando.

"What do you mean?" he says. "Part of democracy."

Let us suppose that Fernando says, "Of the democratic party system. Of the regime."

"I'm talking about democracy, not the regime," Aramburu says firmly.

"We already know what all of you mean by democracy, General. When it's tame, you respect it. When it's not, you overthrow it. Like Perón."

"Perón wasn't democracy," Aramburu says. "At least, not how I conceive it."

"How do you conceive it?" another companion asks. He's sitting at the table eating. He doesn't say much. His name will not be recorded. Nobody knows who he is, who he was. It's no matter: we know he was there. We would, if we wanted, choose a name for him. There is no reliable story for what we are narrating. And there won't be. There are only privileged narrators. Especially Firmenich. He was there and he offered one version of the history. But he often contradicts himself clumsily. He says that Aramburu was gagged when they took him down into the cellar where Abal will kill him. Later he forgot to say that they took the gag out. Or they didn't take it out or there was no gag. But, how can a gagged man say *proceed*? So we'll identify as "Julio" this character they call *comrade*. In any case, he doesn't say much. And probably from here on out he speaks less than not much. One or two words. Probably he doesn't talk. Nevertheless, he's said something important.

"How do you conceive it?" he asks. Perhaps ironically. Because everybody knows that the democracy Aramburu conceives of is not like theirs. Better yet, they don't give a damn about democracy. They have good reason: they never knew it, it was only a word spoken by the regime to justify its denials and trample the rights of the people. The Yanquis also always go around spouting this word. And they're the Yanquis. The ones who, according to Che Guevara, are the enemy of the human race.

"I'm talking about a democracy no one knows," Aramburu says. "One new to this country. One neither you nor I have ever lived."

Gaby has sat down in front of a typewriter. What kind is it? An Olivetti, a Remington? Let us suppose it is a Lettera 32. Does she write the communiqués or were they already written? It would be usual for them to have already been written. No one can write the future. Or foretell it in COMMUNIQUÉS. Probably— it's *one* possibility—it's Ramus who has gone from La Celma to the house where Norma is and has returned. Who moves around without our knowing very well where. Probably he's the one who has informed her about the development of events. Gaby types up the first communiqué or gives final form to the outline Fernando had already written. The result is what follows:

PERÓN RETURNS

COMMUNIQUÉ NO. I

TO THE PEOPLE OF THE NATION:

Today at 9:30 AM, our Command operation proceeded to detain Pedro Eugenio Aramburu, fulfilling an order stemming from our procedure to submit him to Revolutionary Justice.

Pedro Eugenio Aramburu is charged with treason to the country and the people and with the assassination of twenty-seven Argentines.

At this time, Aramburu represents a player in the regime that has the goal of putting him in power to deceive the people once again

with a false democracy and legalize the handover of our country.
In due course, details of the trial and the sentence passed will be
released. At such a sad time for our Argentina, which sees its governments auctioned off to the highest bidder by its leaders, who enrich
themselves immorally at the expense of the poverty of our people,
we the Montoneros call for armed resistance against the government
of right-wing thugs and oligarchs, following the example of General
Valle and all those who generously gave their lives for a Free, Just,
and Sovereign Fatherland.

PERÓN OR DEATH! LONG LIVE THE FATHERLAND!

JUAN JOSÉ VALLE COMMANDO OPERATION

MONTONEROS

Gaby leans back in her chair. She looks over the text. She can't
believe it. Shit. They did it! The uproar this is going to produce in
the country. The journalistic toadies in the newsrooms are going
to shit their pants when they read this communiqué. It will be
passed from hand to hand. They won't know if it's authentic or
not. Or worse—if it's authentic, they're not going to have the guts
to publish it. And if they do, they're going to be scared for their
lives.

Arrostito is not wrong. The communiqué makes the whole
country tremble. Years later, in the midst of the terror of the Videla regime, another text will show up in the newsrooms: Rodolfo
Walsh's *Letter to the Military Junta.* It didn't upset anyone. At
the magazine *Gente,* they passed it around laughing so hard they
choked. Get a load of this crazy! Who does he think he is? Him
alone against the military junta. The commanders must be trembling in their boots. That Irishman was always a little crazy. By

now they should have put him in an oven. That magazine was full of "voluntary hangmen for Videla." There are many ways to kill someone. When the army finds it necessary to produce the death of Arrostito, *Gente* will publish a cover that is studied and will be studied as an impeccable example of the banality of evil. There's a photograph of Gaby and, covering it partially, a bureaucratic stamp, an office stamp applied with a heavy hand, with brutality. The printed word is "Dead."

But Communiqué no. 1 from the Montoneros makes everyone shudder.

Things are grave.

Over at *Gente* it's possible they've repeated a phrase that years ago caused the kidnapping of a foreign ambassador in Guatemala: *What must we make of ourselves in order to survive?*

Exactly what they did make of themselves.

To her misfortune, few had to discover it as fully as Gaby.

After the "Aramburu blow," she got turned into a myth. That explains why she ended up staying so long in the ESMA Navy dungeon. Her torture is drawn out because they don't want to kill her. She's a trophy. The navy shows her off with pride. They've got her. They got the "cunt" of the Montoneros. That how they put it: the *cunt* of the Montoneros. There are secret histories that entrap her and give her surprising leading roles. So as, in 1974, Perón, seeking to disarm the Montonero Leadership, tells Juan Manuel Abal Medina he wants to talk to her. But how to find her? Also, can Perón, in 1974, talk to Norma Arrostito without his men, that powerful neofascist circle that he strengthened, preventing it? Can there be anything crazier for Perón, just months from his death, than talking with Gaby?

Aramburu continues, "Perón's democracy was incomplete: it marginalized the anti-Peronistas. So was that of the anti-Peronistas: it marginalized Perón, and it marginalized you."

"Excuse me, but it's not the same thing," Fernando says. "Democracy is the government of the majority."

"As far as the minorities are concerned."

"I'm sorry to hear you use that phrase," Fernando says, shaking his head in disagreement. "That's pure liberal garbage. Democracy is the government of the people. And the minorities, the stinking minorities, do not want the people to govern. Perón always had the minorities against him. The oligarch and the thuggish sector of the army. You, for example. Just ask yourself this: Can a popular government respect the minorities?"

"If it can't respect them, then there's no democracy."

"Just ask yourself this: Is there any time when the minorities respected the people? No, never. Minorities are not interested in democracy. Just review the history of these past fifteen years. Why don't you grant democracy? Because you'll lose. You'll have to have free elections and the people will not vote for you. You'll lose, General. That's why Perón is in Madrid. Why Peronismo is banned. Why we're fed up. Why you're here. On trial."

Aramburu has listened to him very calmly, as though only

waiting for the break that will allow him to go on. Perhaps we should point out that he has hesitated to say that any dialogue between him and his kidnappers is impossible. Perhaps—and we shouldn't forget this—he continues trying to buy time.

"What we never had," he says firmly, like a man who believes in his words, "was democracy for everyone. Peronistas and anti-Peronistas. A Congress that included all the parties. A state that governs through its three branches. Transparent elections. Without fraud, without prohibitions. That's the democracy I envision."

"It's going to be hard for you to understand, General," Fernando says. "But that democracy of yours is what makes you the most dangerous man in Argentina. As far as we're concerned, you understand. Have you spoken yet with Perón?"

"Not yet. But I have the best contacts. People who are faithful, honorable. Who hold me in esteem. Who respect him. We're going to talk at any moment."

"How touching. Look," Firmenich says, showing his buck teeth, which never seem to fit quite right in his mouth. "The enemies of tomorrow are today's allies."

"What's wrong with that?" Aramburu says. "You've got to have grandeur in politics. Great men . . ."

"Don't be stupid," Fernando says, raising his voice. "You're not a great man."

"Young man, don't forget to whom you are speaking."

"I know very well whom I'm talking to."

"I demand respect. I'm General Aramburu. Of course you know to whom you're speaking. On the other hand, I don't even know if your names are Juan or Pedro."

"Nor will you know."

"Let's go back to the question of democracy," Julio says. Why not? If he is a comrade, if he's here, he must have said something. It's a third voice: Fernando, Firmenich, and him. Every now and then, when he returns, Ramus. Different versions mention Capuano Martínez, Ignacio Vélez. They are not part of this story. No one knows if they were there. There was someone who was called "the other comrade." Here he's called "Julio." We can't take him lightly. He has suddenly led the dialogue back to its main point: democracy. He's not successful.

Aramburu brusquely changes the subject. He says something unexpected. He surprises his interrogators. "And tell me. Perón—is he a great man?"

"Perón is a great leader of the masses. You've got to have greatness for that. The people do not elect leaders of clay," Fernando says.

"I disgree with you there. The people make mistakes. Do you have a cigarette?"

"You smoke?"

"When I'm about to get killed, yes."

"No one said we were going to kill you."

"Then forget the cigarette."

Fernando stands up and walks slowly around the table. The meal is over. It probably went on longer than was reasonable. But there's something he doesn't want to let go of.

"It's just like you to say that the people make mistakes," he says. "Very like someone accustomed to govern without the people. Or against them."

"That would make for a long discussion."

"Are you in any hurry?"

"What do you think? No one's heard anything from me. My poor wife, for example. Have you thought about her? Doesn't anyone else exist for you? She must be out of her mind."

"Let's go back inside," Fernando says.

Aramburu is seated on the bed. Sitting there like that, with no jacket, with exhaustion of the day showing on his face, the wrinkles that stand out in deep furrows—especially the two that extend down from the sides of his mouth, the two that give him the look of bitterness—with his sad eyes, his pants wrinkled, sitting there like that, he doesn't look like Aramburu. But he is. And everything that is transpiring in La Celma Ranch and everything that is likely to transpire as a consequence is because he is. And even if he wanted, even if he is more and more certain that because he is it will mean death, there is no going back; he cannot cease to be who he is.

"Perón is not going to make any deal with you," Firmenich says.

"Not if you kill me."

"You talk about death more than we do."

"It's very simple: if someone here has got to die here, it's me. I'm all alone. I'm unarmed." He changes topics, as though talking about something so obvious did not interest him. He says, "Where'd you get the idea Perón won't make a deal with me?"

"General, the democracy you propose is of the bourgeois kind," Fernando says. "The democracy of the regime. Peronismo is not the regime. You're never going to make it a part. To do so, you'd have to refute yourselves. Disappear. You represent the classes that exploit. Perón, those who are exploited. The working class. There is no deal possible."

"Perón made a deal. During his first government, the workers and the upper classes got along. Then he lost his way."

"Exactly," Firmenich says. "Because the way is not concilia-tion. Perón knows that now. The only way is that of anti-imperialist national revolution. The destruction of the oligarchy and the army of toads. There is no other way, General."

"Perón told you that?"

"We've not spoken with him yet," Julio says. Does he have the authority to reveal something like that? Difficult to know. It would be better to give a line like that to Fernando.

"We haven't spoken to him yet," Fernando says.

"You didn't tell me that. Anyway, we know what Perón's like. If you speak with him, he'll tell you what you need to hear him say."

"Does he do that to you?"

Aramburu thinks about it. He scratches his nose. Suddenly, he sneezes. He rubs his face with a hand.

"It's possible. But only if I throw Onganía out. If I organize a government of national unity. If I call Perón, he will come."

"That's why you're so dangerous for us, General," Firmenich says. "If you accomplish what you say, Peronismo as a revolu-tionary force dies. Because it's for sure that Perón is up there in years. And if you offer him redress. The uniform. And clean elec-tions, maybe he'll come. And consolidate the democracy of the regime. We're here to keep that from happening."

"The people don't want a tie-and-jacket revolution," Julio says, sure of his words this time. "They want a Peronismo that will make a revolution. Just like Evita asked for."

"May I ask you something?" Aramburu says. They all continue to look at him seriously. Aramburu feels like he has the right to ask, "How do you know what the people want? How come you speak in their name with so much certainty? If this ranch belongs to one of you, let me tell you that the people do not have ranches. And that you are not part of them."

"You're talking stupid, General," Fernando says, enraged. "We are a vanguard group. Neither Lenin nor Trotsky nor Che were proletarians. But they knew what the people wanted. Because, by contrast with you and your comrades, they listened to the people, were familiar with their suffering and the exploitation you subject them to. That cute little speech you direct at those of us who have more than ten pesos in our pockets, saying we can't understand the people because we're not poor, is an insult. And a dumb thing to say."

"I think this is a conversation between deaf men," Aramburu says, exhausted for the first time.

"Possibly," Firmenich says. "But you should know this, General: there will be no democracy with the regime. There will be no tie-and-jacket Peronismo. Peronismo will never be assimilated. Peronismo and the regime do not go together. We proletarians are always going to demand wages you will not or cannot pay. Cannot is only a figure of speech. Because you can if you want to. What you can't do is reduce the margin of profits. Capitalist greed."

Aramburu leans back against the wall. He's sorry he didn't do so before. He wouldn't be so tired now. He was held back by that dignity of military men who trust in everything straight. Standing tall, looking straight ahead, rifle on your shoulder, eyes on the flag, up in the sky. Never loosening up. Wearing underwear two sizes too small does a good job of squeezing your balls, and you raise your head and hold your gaze on high. Like Belgrano standing by the Paraná River. And that's why we've got a flag.

"What I wouldn't give to have Perón here," Aramburu says, out of the blue.

"So would we," Firmenich says. We kidnapped you so we could bring Perón back."

"Don't get me wrong," Aramburu says. "I mean here *right now.* Here, with us. We could ask him a few questions. Or two. Just two. For example . . ." He stops. It's evident he wants to find the exact formulation for the two questions. It's not easy. It's hard for him to come up with his captors' question. He's been listening to them for hours. He's learned something about their language. He knows they're not Marxists or communists. They're Peronistas. They're Christians. And also—and this facet upsets him, because at times it gives him hope, but at times it makes him lose it completely—they're idealists. They're not mercenaries. They obey no one. They belong neither to Onganía nor to Imaz. That would be beyond belief. They are too refined; you can tell they're educated. Their families must be honorable people, upper class. But idealism is the secret force of fanatics. There is no greater idealist than a fanatic. No one like a fanatic embodies the certain, intimate need and legitimation to kill.

"For example?" Firmenich is getting impatient.

"You would ask him, General, would you like to lead a national revolution? Would you like to bring together in a definitive way the working class and the oligarchy? Would you like to break off relations with the United States? Would you like . . . ?"

"That's a lot of questions," Fernando interrupts.

"It's only one: Would you like to lead a national revolution? Perón would understand what that means."

"What would you ask him?"

"Perón . . ."

"That's a bad start. You forgot to give him back his rank."

"Perón and I know each other. I called him *Perón* and he called me *Aramburu*."

"Let it go. Go on."

"Perón, would you like to head up a legitimate democracy based on all citizens voting, wearing your general's uniform and free of all charges that have been levied against you?" Strangely, Aramburu smiles and looks at them like he's triumphed. The response of the Montoneros comes right back.

"You don't know the General," Fernando says. "You know very well that today the people would only follow him if he heads up an anti-imperialist revolution. That's what he represents today. Whether you like it or not, that's what he's got to do. Latin America is living revolutionary times. The Cuban Revolution, General. No popular leader can offer less without it costing him as such. We're not stupid. What Perón thinks is not important. What is important is what he represents objectively and what he has to accept. No one can be Perón today and not be a revolutionary. Because that's what the people and History expect of him."

"Another Castro?"

"But one who's Argentine," Firmenich says. "Revolution has gone a long way in Latin America. If Perón returns, he's got to be a part of it. With his story, with the love he has for the masses, there is no other choice. And believe me, General: that's what Perón must do. Because he's alive. Because he's an artisan of History. He works with the materials he has at hand. What he has at hand now is a people and an uncontainable ideology: socialism."

"You don't know Perón."

"You're the one who doesn't know him," Firmenich says. "And we understand him. All you can do is look at him with your narrow ideology of a soldier. As a man of order."

Aramburu smiles. It's as though he knew something these youngsters couldn't help but ignore—for the simple reason that they're youngsters, and what's more, because they are not part of the military. And finally, because they had never gone head to head with Perón. A late-afternoon dialogue in the stillness of the officers' club when they, military men, because they get up so early, are already starting to get sleepy.

"Get this straight and then do what you want. I, the right-wing thug Aramburu, am not half the military man Perón is. Perhaps my ideology is smaller than his. Perón is the intelligent type of soldier. He taught at the Escuela de Guerra. He read Clausewitz carefully. But he's more of an anticommunist than I am, guys. And he likes order as much as we all do. As all military men do. We are children of order and we are taught to defend it. Believe me if you want to. If not, prepare yourselves to be surprised."

May 31 is the last day of the trial. Aramburu knows only one topic is left—the most difficult one. The one that scares him the most.

Fernando Abal Medina says, "Let's talk about Eva Perón."

What could he tell them about Evita? Could they, snot-nosed kids between twenty and twenty-three years old, understand something he might explain to them? *Do you pretend to know her? I saw her up close, I saw her walk, I saw her sit down, stand up. I shook her hand innumerable times. I saw her very expensive clothes, her shoes. I heard her speak, I saw her smile—I never saw her cry. Then I saw her hair bun, that tailored suit she wore like a uniform, like a soldier in battle. I saw her begin to die and I saw her almost dead. I saw her become pallid. I saw her lose her curves and the splendid, beautiful health in her face. She sprouted cheekbones like rocks. Her lips grew thin. Even her ankles grew thin, because they were always thick and that was a torment for her. You could see the bones in her hands. Her voice grew harsh. It seemed all she did was give orders. Until she died.*

Then, despite the circus Perón set up, I see the people really crying for her. I'm going to tell you about Evita's people. There was no question they loved her. Willingly, humbly, and even submissively— without shame, without honor. You can't love a person that way. There's no room left to love yourself. No pride left. I saw the people turn themselves over to that love to the point of losing themselves, losing all presence, to the point of immolation. If you'd asked them what they were—what they were, you see—they might have said,

*"We are our love for Evita." That's how she was able to manipulate
them however she wanted. I know you will say, "They went so far in
their love for her because of the hatred with which all of you treated
them. That was the first time anyone loved them. How could they
not give in to it? How were they not going to love Eva to the point
of not loving themselves?" I know what you will say: "They were full
of love. Never had a people loved so much. How could it matter to
them to give her all their love if they had hers? They did not have to
love themselves because she loved them. That was sufficient. That
was enough." As you can see, I have thought about this question.
But there's another aspect.*

Aramburu will never tell them what he means by *another
aspect*. Aramburu thinks that the people loved Eva so much
because they were ignorant. Because they were mestizos who
had just come in from the countryside. "Black heads," "greasers,"
as she called them. An educated people can't love a government
official that way. An educated people never loses their critical dignity. No one can go overboard, drown himself in someone else.
Only a country of animals, fanatics, could go to such extremes
for love. What can you expect from such a people? Too much,
the worst. The love of fanatics sweeps everything away with it.
There are no decrees possible in the face of the passions of the
ignorant. Someone who hasn't been polished, burnished by culture will only treasure passion, the fury of the barbarous. *I know
they're going to ask me why we hid her. What did they expect? That
we would let them keep their dead saint? And what's worse, a dead
saint that was vengeful, tempestuous, bellicose? No, we weren't crazy. Evita, in Argentina, would have made the country blow sky-high.
She would have been a flash point for every rebellion. The altar of*

every hatred. We would have spent all our time cleaning the flowers up from her tomb, only to start all over again the next day. And the next. And the next. The priests of the people would have gone there. They would have celebrated their tempestuous masses. The most fanatical would have lived their lives waiting for her to arise from her tomb to lead them into battle, to triumph. We would have had to beat them with clubs. Or kill them. They would be trying me now for many other deaths. Not for Valle's and his companions. Not for the ones in the José León Suárez garbage dump. For many others. For the deaths of mountains of other dirty niggers, fanatics, unworthy of an educated country like this one. We had already put up with her alive. Fortuntely, she went quick. To put up with her dead would have been madness. I know they now will ask me where she is. Who knows why they would want her now. To turn her over to the people. To initiate a grand uprising of the people with the body of the Bitch as a flag. No, not a word about that. I'm not going to betray my country. Nor my own people. Keep the Whore far away.

Arrostito expected something like that. The services never sleep. They react immediately. Various "communiqués" appeared from "armed organizations." Aramburu had been kidnapped by half the world. A painful, but no less unexpected, bit of information needs to be added. A pack of jerks, adventurers must have set a trap with rotten meat to produce such an uproar. The country is in flames. No one knows a thing. But the "heroes" continue to crop up. From the right, from the left. It's necessary to put a stop to it. Shut their mouths. They can't tell the truth yet, can't say, "We were the ones." We are an armed group of Christians and Peronistas and we offed Aramburu. Anyone else going around spewing communiqués is lying. The truth, and not only in this matter, belongs to us. For now, Gaby decides to write another communiqué.

PERÓN RETURNS

COMMUNIQUÉ NO. 2

To the people of the Nation:

In the face of the publication of false communiqués attributed to armed organizations proclaiming the arrest of Pedro Eugenio Aramburu and laying down conditions for his ransom, the Leadership of our Organization finds itself obliged to make clear the following declarations:

1) On May 29, at 9:30 AM, our Juan José Valle commando force proceeded to arrest Pedro Eugenio Aramburu.

2) In order to demonstrate the veracity of this affirmation, we provide the following details:

a) Pedro Eugenio Aramburu is carrying no documentation on his person.

b) The personal effects on his person included a keychain in the form of a medallion with the inscription "The Fifth Infantry Regiment to Gen. Pedro Eugenio Aramburu, May 1955; two Parker ballpoint pens; a plasticized calendar from the Interior Bank; a handerchief; a gold tie pin; and an automatic wristwatch.

c) He was arrested in the dining room of his home.

3) Due to the nature of the charges that occasioned the arrest of Pedro Eugenio Aramburu, with the intent to subject him to Revolutionary Justice, there is no chance of negotiating his release with the regime.

4) We request that organizations whose names have been circulated to make a quick disclaimer of their false communiqués.

PERÓN OR DEATH! LONG LIVE THE FATHERLAND!

MONTONEROS

"I don't have much to say about that. Others took care of it."

Firmenich shakes his head. He takes his time to say, "We don't believe you. Everything went through your hands."

Aramburu pretends to be surprised. "With Rojas there with me? Given the hatred the vice presidency had for the Navy?"

"Rojas wasn't able either to do anything you had no knowledge of," the other comrade—the one we have decided to call "Julio" —says.

Aramburu says, "I would appreciate a cigarette."

"This is a trial," Fernando says. "You can't smoke here. Where's Eva?"

Aramburu appears to lose his patience. "What is this obsession with Evita?" he says, crossly. "You didn't even know her. You're youngsters from powerful families. I don't think you owe her anything. Not a home. Not a toy. Not a bottle of cider and a piece of bread. The sort of things to win over the simple hearts of the poor."

"There are answers we could give for these insults you're muttering," Fernando says. "General, the hearts of the poor are not so simple. And you can't buy them with cider and hunks of bread. I insist: Where is Eva?"

"Why do you want her?"

"The Peronista nation wants her."

"And you'll turn her over to them?"

"Tell us where she is and we'll do that. She's not ours. She belongs to them."

"She belongs to Perón."

"Perón and the people are one and the same. If we give her to Perón, we are giving her to the people. If we give her to the people, she will rest in the same hands as Perón's. That's what we want. Her rest."

"She's resting. We gave her a Christian burial."

Fernando looks at him furiously. His eyes shine when he looks like that; he furrows his brow, and his face goes tense. He grits his teeth.

"You have a strange idea of a Christian burial," he says. "You give a Christian burial when their own people bury them, their family members, their friends, their comrades. Not their enemies. When a priest speaks words from the Gospels. A priest chosen by the family. When the body has been waked during a long night in which no one has slept. When the hands that raise the casket are those of family members or those of friends and brothers brought together by grief."

"We couldn't bury Eva Perón in Argentina. You've got to understand that."

"If you die, you'll be buried in Argentina."

"It's not the same thing, Fernando." It's the first time Aramburu has used his name. He's sorry he did: it's one more demonstration of how, if he lives, he will denounce them with full details. Their names, their clothes, their faces, the tone of their voices.

I'm not going to get out of this, he thinks. But he goes on: "I am a retired military man. Eva is a myth. A cult. A religious object. She can convoke multitudes."

"Which you would have to kill."

"Repress."

"Repress for you means kill."

"I don't agree. You make us look like monsters. What a remarkable country, isn't it? You think the same thing about us that we think about you. Do you know how many radicals, conservatives, and communists Perón's police tortured? How many Catholics like you? During the last days of the regime. At the time of the conflict with the Church. Young Catholics were opposed to him then."

"Not now."

"Yes, and that's hard for me to understand. But I've changed, so why not you? That's what's strange: we changed in the same way. Going over to Peronismo. I didn't become a Peronista, but I want to understand it. Why can't we understand each other, then?"

"Because of the past."

"The past is behind us. No one wants to go there. What's dead is dead. It's time to . . ."

"Spare us the schoolbook talk," Firmenich interrupts very quickly. "You've not left the past behind. You want to bring it up to date. Assimilate what you couldn't destroy into the regime. But your intentions are always the same: those of the regime's, with Peronismo now a part. With your right-wing thug intelligence, you're our most dangerous enemy."

A shadow comes over Aramburu's face. Suddenly he is a man who has understood everything. The complete, entire totality of the question.

"If the best I have to offer you makes me the most dangerous of your enemies, why bother to go on talking, gentlemen? Pass your sentence and shoot me right now."

The next day they interrogate him without the tape recorder. Aramburu's beard has grown out even more. This marks him even more than the wrinkles. And his cheeks are completely sunken, like two bags that hang down and sadly frame his face. He doesn't seem like he is much disposed to fight. His judges are fresh. They haven't shaved, either, but they have less beard. It's a detail that the leader whom they are defending today will use years later to disparage them: *peach fuzzes,* he'll call them.

"Do you want to go on talking about Evita?" he asks.

"We ask the questions, General," Firmenich says. "No matter how hard it is for you to believe it—even though, as you can see, we are not surrounded by the solemn carnival with which the bourgeoisie adorns justice—you are here before a tribunal."

"I know all too well. I only hope that that justice will be fair."

"More than the bourgeoisie's, without question. It is not in the service of the oligarchy, the corporations or imperialism. It is in the service of . . ."

"The people. I already know that. You've already forbid me to make schoolbook speeches. Spare me your revolutionary speeches."

Firmenich smiles slyly. Let us suppose that he thinks, *Right-wing shit. You think you can still lord it over us. I know what you*

*must think, that we're a bunch of assholes and the cops are going
to show up any minute and rescue you. We're going to shit in our
pants and take you back home, safe and sound, to your wife and
your slippers.*

Nevertheless, the hope of salvation is receding from Aramburu. He no longer looks to win some time. He can see they've
not been successful in finding him. Or Onganía's police is not
working very hard at it. That certainty closes in on him hour after
hour: Why would Onganía want to save him? Leper-Lip must
know the whole story. Serenity and false alarms have been his
words to the wise. But his friends? And those who were with him
in the patriotic act of overthrowing him? Nothing but complete
incompetents. They will have denied everything. They will not
have allowed them to take part in anything. They're left leader-
less, right? Screw yourselves, without Aramburu, there is no
overthrow. There is no replacement. Onganía stays on. Twenty or
thirty more years—just like he said.

"General, for the last time, where is Evita?" Fernando asks.
"The tape recorder is still turned off. Whatever you say stays
here."

Aramburu takes a deep breath and loudly lets his breath out.
He says, "She's in a cemetery in Rome. Don't ask me which one.
There's more than one cemetery in Rome. I know that Eva Perón
is in one of them. I don't know which one."

Fernando runs his hand over his head, as though grooming
himself. It's impossible to comb that shiny hair, held in place by
gel. But that gesture allows him to win a few seconds. What he
thought in those few seconds was terrible. The idea crossed his
mind like a tornado. He told Aramburu, "General, I'm going to

level with you. This is the moment, the exact moment, in which
a prisoner is subjected to torture. Let us review the situation:
you say that Eva Perón is in a cemetery in Rome. We need to
know which one. It's of utmost importance for our organization
to know that. If we know it, in less than two days the body of
the standard-bearer of the humble, the most beloved woman in
Argentina, will be in our hands. In that case we can talk to Perón.
We become miraculous. We can obtain what no one could. The
regime respects us. The people love us. Perón needs us. As you
will see, the motives for obtaining that information are powerful. You're telling us, 'Don't ask me what cemetery Eva Perón is
in.' We ask ourselves, 'Why? Why aren't we going to ask you that
question? What prevents us?' You prevent us. You, who says, 'I
know she's in some cemetery. I don't know which one.' And what
if we don't believe you? You will observe that you place yourself
too close to the truth. Rome, cemetery in Rome, there's more
than one, but not too many, Eva Perón is in one of them. You
know all that. What you don't know is very little. The only thing
you don't know is in which cemetery. Do you not know it, or are
you refusing to tell us? Tell me, General, how do we solve that
problem?"

"By means of torture."

"Exactly."

"I know a few things about torture," Aramburu says. "They
could be useful to you."

"Keep talking. But I want to establish one thing. I've already
taken my stand on the matter. Nothing you say can change it."

While this sentence upsets him, Aramburu does not stop.
He develops his theory: "I distrust the efficacy of torture. I don't

mean to say it doesn't have results. If it didn't, it wouldn't be an option with so much abusive frequency. But let's look at it, nevertheless: the torturer supposes the person being tortured is in possession of a truth he wishes to know. To extract from him. That's why he tortures him. The person being tortured may or may not have that truth in his possession. If he does and is courageous. . . . Courageous here, if you will allow me, only means he can tolerate the pain."

"Don't you think the strength of one's convictions helps in tolerating pain?" Firmenich asks, intervening in the dialogue.

"Yes, but it can also go against him. I'm not talking about *any* kind of torture. I am talking about the kind you are tempted to subject me to."

"OK, but why talk in the abstract when we're in the most concrete of situations?" Fernando says.

"Let us suppose you torture me. Let us suppose that I am courageous. That I tolerate the pain because I believe so deeply in the cause I represent. We'll both fail, then. You, because you don't get the information. I, because I am so courageous, end up dying under torture. You have one thing and not the other, precisely the one you want. You have my body but not my truth. I have not told you. Let us look at another point of view. You torture me and I, who cannot tolerate the pain beyond a certain point, tell you where Eva Perón is buried. But I die. I confessed, but I held out too long. I confessed when it was too late. When you could no longer revive me. That's a problem for you. It's always a problem for the torturer when the person being tortured dies. Did I tell the whole truth? Did I keep something back? Did I die too soon? Did I die before confessing everything? Is what you got enough? Let's go on to another aspect of the question. It's almost the most common and cruelest one. Here is where the torturer usually attains the limits of his barbarianism."

"Of his inhumanity," Fernando says. But then he quickly corrects himself: "If it's true we consider torture inhumane. I would say it's a completely human art. Every now and then we say someone's an animal, either for their ignorance or for their brutality. I'm tired of hearing that the torturer sinks into bestiality when he tortures. That's false. Animals don't torture. Go on, General. You are managing to entertain us."

"That's not my intention."

"What is, then?"

"Let's continue," Aramburu says. "What's the new aspect of the question? The one I defined as the most common and the cruelest. It's simple: *the person being tortured has nothing to offer.* He does not possess the *truth* that the torturer requires. This brings us to the limits of the horror. If the torturer believed the person being tortured, it would not be this way. But, to his enormous misfortune, the person being tortured is never successful in being as convincing as the torturer requires. Besides, when the torturer begins his task, it's hard to stop him. The situation can prolong itself indefinitely. The torturer, in torturing him, demands from the person being tortured a truth he believes him to harbor. But that's not the way it is. The person being tortured does not have what the torturer needs. Except that the torturer doesn't believe it. This gets resolved in two ways. Although in the end it winds up always being one and the same thing. First way: the only thing the person who is being tortured can do is to *lie*. If I don't have the truth you demand from me, but I can't convince you that I don't have it, all that is left for me to do is to invent it. Here, the person being tortured lies. Second way: the torturer doesn't belive him—either because he wishes to go on torturing him, or because the truth the person being tortured offers is of no use to him. Or because he discovers that the person being tortured is making it up, inventing it. At this point, he's becoming delirious. The torture continues without stopping. It continues right up to the end. The person being tortured dies. The torturer is left empty-handed. And there's another possibility. The simplest one. You decide to torture me. But I can't tolerate the pain. Suffering terrifies me. The offense to my body. Almost certain death. I confess without your torturing me. I make a complete confession. You have triumphed. You have what you want: the truth I was protecting. And you have a healthy enemy. An enemy you despise. Nothing is more despicable than a coward. So you kill me. Or not. Perhaps you set me free. I return home. I retreat into my room. I shoot myself. I cannot live with my cowardice."

"In all four cases, the person being tortured dies," Fernando says.

"That's right," Aramburu says.

"When did you think this all up?"

"I've seen too many people tortured. Under Perón. Under the government of the overthrow. Especially, as you might imagine, at the hands of the Navy. Under Frondizi's CONINTES. And in other countries, too. I was able to draw some conclusions."

"What other countries, General? Although we have our suspicions."

"You're going to have them confirmed. I was in Algeria in 1959. I spent a whole week talking to a general from OLAS. He taught me all these theories about torture. He had a pitiless position with regard to the person being tortured: he should never survive. Then I was in the School of the Americas. The French are superior. The Yanquis don't know how to handle the psychological question. They massacre the person being questioned and that's it. I believe, nevertheless, they are more efficient than the French. I have a couple of other theories to share with you, but I don't want to bore you. You must know how to torture; you probably have your own methods. Despite the French and the Americans, believe me when I say I came to many of the theories on my own. The topic interests me."

"There's one you haven't come to, General," Fernando says. "If you told us the theories you have developed, it's so we wouldn't torture you. To get us to understand that in any one of the possible cases, you would die. You suppose we don't want that. And you're right. We can't want that *now*. The tribunal hasn't even met. But there's something you missed, that you didn't take into account. That you don't know. How could you take it into account if you are completely unfamiliar with it? Listen, General Aramburu: you are not going to be tortured. Because there's *another* point of view on torture. I already told you: it's ours. I also told you: nothing you might say will change that. And that point of view is the refusal to torture. Our organization does not torture, General. The Montoneros do not torture. If it took torture for you to tell us where Eva Perón is, we would feel unworthy of her. As you know, the torturer is a base, miserable human being. He always ends up hating himself. We are Catholics, General. We believe in God. We are trying you for crimes you committed. We don't want to commit them ourselves."

Ramus arrives for the trial. He knows he's got to be there. He has come and gone many times from the capital. He's missed a lot of it, most of it. But he knows he fulfilled his part. Someone had to establish the link between Timote and the monster of a thousand heads, that city in which everything took on immense, imposing dimensions.

"It's an infernal mess," he describes. "Nobody knows a thing. Everybody knows everything. The cops are all running crazy all over the place. Onganía doesn't know what to do. He knows that this is falling on his head. Everyone's going to think he's the one principally responsible. Directly or indirectly, but principally. He's either an assassin or inefficient."

They remain in the dining room. Seated around the table they look like what they claim to be, what they are certain they are: a revolutionary tribunal in session.

"I'll be right back," Fernando says.

"We're all ready," Firmenich says. "We'll begin whenever you want."

"That's what I'm saying. We're beginning."

Fernando goes into the bedroom. Aramburu is tied to the bed. He shows his hands to Fernando. He asks, "Is this necessary? Do you think I'm going to escape. I don't even know where I am."

"Half the country is looking for you, General. You know that.

Don't ask for something we can't do."

"Anyone can do anything, if he wants. It's not that you can't. It's that you don't want to."

"Do the bonds bother you?"

"What bothers me is being here."

"Don't complain. We're not treating you badly."

"You think so? Dragging me out of my home, bringing me here, interrogating me, and my not knowing if you're going to kill me like a dog or if you're going to toss me out somewhere alive, in the middle of nowhere—what's that? Treating me well?"

"Better than you treated Valle."

"Are you so sure? If my wife wanted to talk to you, what would you tell her? That I'm sleeping. You couldn't ever tell her that. The poor woman doesn't know where you are. Where I am. No one knows. Valle's knew where to go to ask for clemency. Mine doesn't even know that."

"General, there are things you don't understand. Or pretend you don't understand. It's more than obvious that your wife shouldn't know where I am. If she did, we'd have half the army surrounding this piece of property, with Onganía in the lead. Give me a break. Don't says such dumb things. We're treating you well. I always address you by your rank. We've fed you. No one has insulted you. You haven't been hurt. Don't complain." He stops. Clears his throat. Stares at the General. Fernando always proceeded the same way: looking at him, staring into Aramburu's eyes, as though trying to make the latter discover in his eyes the severe certainty of his actions. He says, dryly, "I've come to talk about something else. The revolutionary tribunal is meeting. We have begun to deliberate."

Aramburu, in a low voice, almost in a whisper—in the attempt to make Fernando, whom he knows to be the head of the
operation, feel that the dialogue he now proposes is only between
the two of them, intimate—says, "Kid, don't be stupid," which
surprises Fernando. Not only has he spoken to him familiarly,
but he also called him *kid*. Assuming, for the first time, a hidden
reality that everyone, up until now, has pretended not to know
from the start. Aramburu is a man up in years, almost an old
man. They are *too* young. Aramburu is a giant of the republic. An
army general. A bronze head of the anti-Peronista country. Why
wouldn't he speak to them familiarly? Why would he, now, call
Fernando a *kid*?

"What did you say?" Fernando asks, and a thick and trembling
vein stands out on his forehead.

"I said for you not to be stupid. I could be your father. Listen
to me: don't ruin your life. Don't weigh your shoulders down
with a cadaver like mine. It will weigh you down a lot. They will
always persecute you. Until they leave you dead. And you're going
to give all of this to Perón? If you bring him back, he'll fuck you."

"Your language, General. You surprise me. Do you feel that
lost?"

"I'm doing it for you, kid. What you're doing is not worth the
trouble. Sacrificing your life this way for the old man of Puerta
de Hierro. I swear I just don't understand it. We knew there were
kids like you. We've spoken on various occasions about you at the
Círculo Militar."

"What an honor."

"What do you want from that scumbag of an old man? He's a
pervert, a scoundrel. He's not worth one of your young lives. Who

filled your head with these ideas? Who made you buy all this nonsense you believe in?"

Fernando does not answer. Aramburu is sweating. He looks upset. You can also see him using his last weapons. If this doesn't work, it's all over. He could tell him worse things about Perón. He could tell him terrible things. Things only he and a few others know. Fernando looks at him impassively, his eyes always fixed on him.

"Kid, what do you know about Perón? Do you want me to tell you about him? Do you want to know what a scumbag you're going to kill me for? I can tell you abominable things about Perón."

"Don't waste your breath, General. I've heard abominable things about Perón for fifteen years. Me and all of us. All the *kids* like me. My entire generation. That's why we stand by him. Do you know who convinced us about all the outlandish things we believe in? You and others like you, General. You made us what we are. You invented us. We're the perfect fruit of the country of thugs. Now, go fuck yourselves."

Aramburu raises his voice. He shakes his bound hands as though trying to free himself—not to escape, but to express with greater vehemence what he will say to Fernando. Let us take note of this: it's an Aramburu we have hardly met, someone with an unexpected passion. No one would have thought that. No one knows, also, what a man will do facing the possibility or the near certainty of impending death. Now, as though spitting at him, he aims furious words at Fernando: "You're going to get fucked. I'm still inventing you, kid. You continue to be what I make of you. Now I've changed you into a kidnapper, a fugitive from the law. If you kill me, I'm going to turn you into an assassin. What's worse, what you want never to forgive me for is turning you into a paid assassin for a dirty old man. You're going to give your young life to a cretin with a heart of ice who doesn't deserve it. I beg you for forgiveness. I condemned you to hell. Nevertheless, you're the one who made all the decisions. You could have acted differently. It didn't have to turn out this way."

"Clear something up for me, General. What is . . . *this*?"

"A mercenary in the service of an old fascist."

"You're talking about me?"

"Yes. Now go fuck yourself."

"Strange that irresponsible, abusive use you right-wing thugs make of the concept of fascist. Perón won two elections legitimately. The majority of the people are behind him, love him, and are waiting for him, knowing that they can trust only in him. That's what you call fascism. You, on the other hand—as repressors of the working class, torturers, executioners, agents of coups, and deniers of democracy—call yourselves democrats and liberators. You send the Peronistas to jail for the act of assembly and raising their voice on behalf of their beloved leader and their venerated saint. You impose grotesque puppet governments. You give them orders as to what they have to do. The minute they deviate, you kick them in the ass. And once again you take charge of things, without a moment's hesitation. You call that democracy? Tell me, General, do you take us for idiots?"

"Try to understand, kid. Is it that hard? You know what it was like to live under Perón? How the hell would you know? Do you know what the Peronista regime was like? We could not allow that garbage to come back: stoolpigeons; block captains; torture; corruption; the irritating personalism; the bronze busts; chang-

ing the names of provinces, streets, avenues; IAPI; that fountain
of spurious transactions; that mechanism for the expropriation
of the earnings of the class that produced the greatness of this
country; the landowners; the legitimate owners of the land; the
bad taste; shameless favoring of industry; the transfer of the earnings of the agrarian sector to the industry—in which, of course,
Perón had his allies; overbearing, runaway unionism; demagogu-
ery; the facile wooing of the masses; class hatred; and, once
again, Fernando Abal. What sums it all up: bad taste. The hicks
in the Colón Opera House. The Peronista March played in the
Colón, and Marianito Mores rather than Toscanini.

"Didn't the people have the right to see the Colón?"

"The Colón wasn't built for the people. Maybe in fifteen or
twenty years a people that has learned to read can have access to
Mozart, Beethoven, and Brahms. Not yet."

"Until then, you're going to keep them out?"

"We can't do that. But it won't be necessary. They're going to
catch on. They're going to stay with Palito Ortega. With Sandro.
They would be bored in the Colón. All they have to do is go one
time and the problem is solved. But you're different, Fernando.
The Colón was created for kids of your class. From good families.
Don't waste it. You belong to a better Argentina. We created it for
you. We cleaned out the provincial separatists, the blacks, and
the Indians for you. Are you going to be ungrateful for that favor?
Tell me, what kind of music do you like?"

"It does not include either Palito or Sandro."

"See, that's what I mean. Another type of blood flows in your
veins."

"Antonio Tormo, Feliciano Brunelli, and Carlos Argentino.

They're the ones I prefer, General."

"Go screw yourself, you shitty brat. You're not going to pull my leg."

"Feliciano Brunelli isn't any worse than Mozart. He's different. If you were to include Mozart in a festival, people would be bored. You put Brunelli on and the dancing, the wine, and the happiness begin. Everything achieves its excellence in the place that belongs to it. It's all music."

Fernando goes over to the door. He stops. Without turning around, he says, "I'll come and tell you when we've reached a verdict after the trial." He turns around abruptly. He looks at him again, and says, "I'll ask you to avoid treating me with familiarity from here on out. If we've stuck to formality up to now, I see no reason to set it aside. Don't call me *kid* again. I'm not your son and you're not my father. You are my prisoner. I have proposed to try you. That and no other is our relationship."

He closes the door.

"The General is clever," Fernando says. "That goes against him. It's strange, isn't it? If he were dimwitted, clumsy, an animal of a military man, it could save his life. But he condemned himself by making use of so many resources. Only someone intelligent could argue with so many fallacies, so many traps, so many sharp arguments, even if they were false, to keep from dying."

Firmenich clucks his tongue in irritation.

"So much phony baloney," he says. "He thinks he can play us for fools. Thinks his age gives him the right. His experience. There're no two ways about it, we have agendas that don't jibe. There is no national unity. No national pacification. They want Perón so they can contain the masses without repression."

Ramus bangs the table. A glass falls and smashes on the floor.

"Calm down, comrade," Firmenich says.

"Calm down like hell. It's all too clear. They can't repress anymore. Not after the Córdoba rebellion. A return by Perón controlled by the regime is the last card they have left to play. There's an ironclad option. They bring him back. Or he's brought back by the Peronista nation. If they bring him back, it's to feed the eternal gum game of national unity. Excuse me, but I shit on national unity. It simply means folding the proletariat into the project of the bourgeoisie as second-class citizens. That runs an enormous risk. But the risk is reduced with Perón. It's business as usual, pure and simple. Let's yield on something so nothing changes. We haven't been able to overcome Peronismo after fifteen years, so let's take it over. It's an old story. If you can't beat them, join them. That's where Aramburu's story's going. We've got ours won."

"The charges," Abal Medina says.

"What charges?" Firmenich says. "We came to Timote having studied the charges in detail. We're not going to start reviewing them now. Let's stop jerking around. The judgment has already been decided. That judgment determined the kidnapping."

Suddenly, the other comrade, "Julio," says something no one's said until then: "We've got to kill him. But for something we haven't said yet. That we haven't made explicit. Our organization needs to come off spectacularly. This is our debut on the Argentine political scene. This is going to give us prestige, power over other armed groups, the people will see us as mythic avengers. We killed the Basque and we avenged Valle and Eva and we blocked the attempt to bureaucratize Peronismo and, overnight, we're celebrities. The whole country is already talking about us. We're the rebellion and we're revolutionary justice. We're young. We're what's new. This will energize the Peronista bases. We have attained our goal."

"The Peronista nation will celebrate," Firmenich says. "The head of the execution squad has paid for his crimes. He deserved it. And he was punished by a bunch of snot-nosed kids who had the balls to do it."

"That's enough," Abal Medina says. "I'll go talk to him."

"Shall we carry the sentence out in the basement?" Ramus asks.

"There's nowhere else," Fernando says. "It's narrow, dark, sordid. But he doesn't deserve better. The comrades in José León Suárez died among piles of garbage. There's no reason to give Aramburu what they didn't have. In any case, he has done better. The men who died at José León Suárez were killed by mercenary cops. Assassins from the system. He is going to be given justice by a revolutionary group. With ideals. By young people who fight on behalf of the people. And for the return of their leader." Fernando stops. He drinks some more Coca-Cola. Then he serves himself a glass of beer. He looks at them one by one. He says with firmness, "I am going to inform him of the sentence."

"Who will execute it?" Ramus asks.

"What do you mean, who?" Firmenich asks, in a voice bordering on rage. "Fernando, of course. We decided that some time ago. He's the one in charge."

"If that was decided some time ago, then why the trial?"

"Listen to me, Carlos. Don't play dumb. What's your point? There wasn't any trial. We only told ourselves what we already knew. Nothing Aramburu said as a counterargument changed our decisions. He was condemned from the moment we decided to kidnap him."

"You came all this way without a single doubt?"

"Not one."

Ramus shrugs his shoulders. *OK, so it's all decided.* Nevertheless, he decides to confess something that will not change a thing, but which he doesn't want to hold back: "There were one or two things I questioned. Not about the bastardly things he did. Not about that. But about what he would say. Something that would show him to be human. To stand before him, to see him.

I don't know if you're following me. One thing is Aramburu as a concept."

"What's that mean?"

"Don't play dumb. You know very well what it means. Aramburu as an idea, jerk. As something abstract. As a thug, as an executioner, as the replacement man for the regime. Another thing is the Aramburu who sat down and ate a meal with us. I looked at his hands. He has his hands done."

"Is that something in his favor?"

"No, but he has a small wound next to one of his ears. Something insignificant. Something from when he shaved. Something that demonstrates that he shaves, that he's like us. A guy who shaves himself in the morning. Or the sad face he shows, the wrinkles, the years on his body. He's no longer an idea. He's flesh and bone and he's sitting there in front of you and you know we're going to kill him. It makes it more difficult. Or when we talk about Evita. What if he tells us where she is? What if he tells us something we don't know? And what if that washes the slate clean with us?"

"Did he say?"

"Does he know? He said he didn't."

"I don't believe him. I think he lied to us." Firmenich takes his time. What he's about to say is complex: "We could have found out. How much pain is Aramburu prepared to tolerate to keep from telling us where Eva is? In my opinion, not a lot."

"You want to torture him?" Fernando asks.

"Lean on him a little bit, at least," Firmenich says, testily.

"A little bit?" Ramus asks. "How much is a little bit? How far does a little bit go? Up to the point at which we begin to become torturers. Where's that line? Who decides?"

Firmenich shakes his head. "You're right," he says. "No one can set that line."

"Enough blabbing," Fernando says grumpily. "We've already discussed these things and decided them in the organization. We don't torture. Period." He drinks a glass of Coke. He downs it all. He clucks his tongue. Then, abruptly, he says, "I'm going to talk to him."

He walks out of the dining room.

Aramburu watches him walk in. What is this hothead going to tell him? He looks more and more like a madman, like a Jacobin. A Jacobin without a people. Without the French Revolution. He invented the Revolution. He can't contain himself. He asks, "So? What did you decide? Are you going to join my project or are you going to sink into the latrines of clandestinity?"

"What a sentence, General," Fernando says with irony. "I'm going to remember it."

"When?"

"Whenever I remember you."

"So you're going to kill me."

"How can you think we'd join your project?"

"Because I can't suppose you want to commit suicide. I'm going to put it to you plain. Even if it's the last time I do it."

"Go ahead and talk. No one is listening. No one will ever know what we say in this room."

"I'm paying for Valle's spilled blood. That's the way history is. A chain of revenge. My blood will demand yours. By killing me you condemn youselves to die, by making them kill you. Someone will avenge me. Don't doubt it for a second. Someone is going to feel he has the same right as you do now. This country still does not know the fury of the Argentine Army. We have an army trained by the OAS and the School of the Americas. If you really knew in detail what's taught there, you would waver."

"We, too, have been trained for war. Not by torturers, but rather revolutionaries. Make no mistake. You are not going to succeed in scaring me. Or making me waver."

"Ask yourself this question. It's the one Gutiérrez de la Concha asked Castelli when the latter was preparing to shoot Liniers. He asked him . . ."

"Don't waste your breath, General. I've known that question for some time. It surprises me you know it."

"That shows your prejudices. You think we military men are animals."

"I could spend the night providing you with proof. Going back to Castelli, he was a lawyer. Gutiérrez de la Concha asked him on the basis of what point of law was he authorized to kill prisoners. A silly question. Castelli was a revolutionary—he and his friend Moreno. They were the law. Every revolution creates its own law. Did you do anything differently? The counterrevolution also makes its own law. Or invalidates those of the revolution."

"Gutiérrez de la Concha had something else to say."

"Come on, General, let's hear it. Did you read it in a children's magazine?"

"I'll overlook that offensive statement. Let's forget Castelli. If you think my quotations come from children's magazines, then I will avoid them. I'll ask you the question."

"I'm all ears."

"You present yourself to me as a revolutionary. You want to change the regime into which I pretend to incorporate Perón. You, on the other hand, want to use Perón to destroy it. Castelli also wanted to change a regime. Executing Liniers was part of that change."

"A substantial part of that change."

"Gutiérrez de la Concha asks him, 'Doctor Castelli, what kind of system is it that starts out like this? What sort of system begins by executing defenseless prisoners?'"

"Don't try to make me misty-eyed, General. Those are all too many arguments to defend just one life—even if it is yours. Gutiérrez was full of crap, if you'll excuse me. A revolution has the right to kill those it wants to get out of the way. If it starts out that way, it starts out on the right foot. You pose for me a question of political ethics. Liberal pap. Any system that begins by killing ends up bad. Is this what you want to propose to me? Aramburu the executioner? Any emergent revolution that does not kill when it has to kill is lost."

"So you're going to kill me."

Fernando doesn't answer. He takes so much time to answer that it seems like an eternity to Aramburu. Then, without solemnity, but with a certain martial air or with harsh clarity, he says, "General Aramburu, the tribunal has sentenced you to death. You will be executed within half an hour."

Aramburu tries to break his bonds. He hurts his wrists. They start to bleed.

"That knot is tightly tied, General," Fernando says. "And even if you succeed in untying it, what would you gain? Your own people have let you down. They haven't found you in time. Have they seriously been looking for you?"

"Who knows? There are a bunch of cretins behind Onganía. People that hate me. Who are repulsed by my plan to negotiate with Perón. They want to see me dead. You are going to do them that favor."

"We, too, are repulsed by your plans to make a deal with Perón. But for other reasons."

"But they match."

"Not at all. They want to uphold the right-wing thug state. We want to destroy it."

"But both of you want to kill me."

"For different reasons. It would be serious if it were for the same ones. You've put yourself in a dangerous position. That of the conciliators. If the two sides don't want to conciliate, they're killed. Crossfire. Although you upset us more than Onganía, the other one who might want your life. You don't want to support the right-wing thug state. You want to create a new regime with Peronismo included. The thugs are animals. They don't even think about that. They only think about getting their repression back. Your plan is more skillfull. It is to turn Perón into a tame general dominated by the bourgeoisie. That'll never happen."

Aramburu again speaks familiarly. He always does when he thinks he is lost, because it's his last card. "You, kid, are an idiot."

"I asked you not to speak familiarly with me. And never to call me *kid*."

"How can I keep from talking to you familiarly when you're a punk? You're going to ruin your life. Your twenty-year-old's idealism is going to cost you dearly. I also was once twenty years old. I also had my youthful dreams. But those dreams didn't require anybody to die."

Fernando looks at him with disdain. Aramburu receives this look straight in the face. Perhaps no one ever looked at him like that. Not with hatred, but as a poor sucker. For the past fifteen years he's been covered in praise, homages, recognitions. But this kid allows himself to look at him scornfully, with a repulsion that is so extreme it wounds and dishonors him. And with a haughtiness, an irreverence that only now appears in a pure state— without the veil, without the forced courtesy between captor and prisoner. That scorn expresses itself ferociously, beyond all civility, any dealings between gentleman, when he says, "General, excuse my frankness. By the time you were twenty years old, you were already a shitty military man with the soul of an assassin."

Fernando turns to leave the room. He's about to grasp the doorknob when Aramburu's deep voice reaches him, holding him back. "You, too, have the soul of an assassin. And all you need is a uniform to be a military man. But, *now,* you don't have one, because when you went to my house you were wearing one. You looked sharp, Fernando. You want to know something? It looked good on you. You liked it. You're only lacking one thing to be a military man through and through. A military man like me. To believe in God. Do you believe in God? What's the matter? Don't you like the question? Does it catch you by surprise? To be sure, it's no good to ask someone if they believe in God when they're about to kill someone. I believe in God, Fernando. I believe that God sees and judges what we do."

"I believe in God. But I don't ask him to see me and judge me."

"You make it easy for yourself. Anyone can do that. A true Catholic feels the weight of God. The look of God. The burden of God on his shoulders. That gives substance to what he's doing. Knowing he's going to be judged by Him, that he's going to have to give Him an account. To Him above all else, Fernando. A Catholic subjects his actions to God more than to any earthly power. He's the one who judges. Not you, not me, not Perón. God, our Lord, is the one who's going to decide if we did good or if we did evil. It is the point in which everything converges. Towards which everything flows. There, in Him, our acts are judged. Especially the acts of those of us who dare to usurp His place by taking the lives of others. God gives and God takes away. Since we cannot give life, we kill. Do you think I don't carry around in my conscience the burden of the death of those you fling in my face? But not for you, for Him. I'm afraid to present myself in a state of sin when He calls me. And you, kid? What do you plan to say to our Lord, to our God, about us Catholics when He asks you why you killed me? There is no greater sin. It represents infinite disobedience. Killing, causing death, is what most alters the order of the Lord. He has said so, Fernando. And if he said so, it was with good reason. Thou shalt not kill. I, who have killed, believing I have that right, bear within me the fear of God. How will He judge that sin? Is He going to pardon me? Is He going to condemn me? Does His Kingdom await me or that of Hell? Haven't you asked yourself that? A Catholic is a man afraid of the judgment of God. If he isn't, he's not a Catholic. He's Perón, who shits on all this. I swear to you he doesn't have any of these problems. Perón has no conscience. He has no spirit. As far as he's concerned, God is a word he uses now and then. I asked him in Paris, 'Do you believe in God?' He smiled cynically, taking it as a joke. He said, 'Why not?' Is that how you would answer if asked the same question?"

"You were with Perón in Paris?"

Aramburu nods. Fernando says, "We heard that story. We never bothered to confirm it. We don't think it flatters him."

"I know. That's why I just told it. I was holding it as a good card. Until I realized that no, it wasn't. Then I put it away."

"Look here a little bit. You and Perón chatting in Paris, drinking a cup of coffee. No two ways about it, it's the capital of love. Did you make up? No. But you explained your plan to him and he said yes, that he agreed. He tells everyone. As far as he's concerned, anyone on his side's a Peronista. He likes to expand. At some point we're going to have to deal with that. You can expand to include both God and the Devil. Saint Teresa and Dracula."

"He thinks he can. And let me tell you, so far he has."

"Now it's easy. The question will be when he returns. Remember what I'm telling you, General. Things'll be different here. Everyone'll be down his throat. And he's going to have to choose."

"I suspect I won't be here to see that spectacle. It's a pity, isn't it? It sounds like it'll be fun."

Fernando smiles. "You're right. If there's something I find wrong with death, it's that it prevents us from continuing to watch the movie. It makes us leave the theater. And for good."

"The only one here who's going to miss still watching the movie is me."

"Don't complain, General. You have the great honor of having premiered it."

He leaves the room.

Don Franco Riganti likes to have his grocery store full of people. Not only because it brings in good money. But also because he feels less lonely. Especially on a Sunday night, like today. He's seated at the head of a large table filled with friends. Don Acébal is sitting next to him. They have eaten and drunk in abundance. Now they are talking about what needs to be talked about. About what everyone's talking about. Because even though no one has heard from Aramburu since Friday, even if all the newspapers, the radio, and TV have blanketed the country with that topic, there's something that interests Don Franco and his friends more. That Sunday, May 31, at 2:30 PM the World Cup began in Mexico. The first match was between Mexico and Russia.

"It makes you mad," a guy in grease-covered overalls says. That's Skinny Artemio and he works in the gas station. He fills cars, checks the carburetor and the oil, knocks tires with a cricket bat, puts water in radiators, and swipes the cars a bit with a feather duster. He almost doesn't do anything else and doesn't know how to. If someone drives up with a serious problem, forget it—unless Artemio calls the owner over. The owner knows more. That's why he's the owner. He's a fat guy who grew up among tools and he even built cars and raced. There's nothing he doesn't know. But he lost a son in a rally. His wife committed suicide. He put on fifty pounds and now he spends the day drinking and taking interminable naps in the office, where there's a desk and a cot all broken down from supporting his weight for so long. Artemio does what he can. But if someone shows up with a problem in the forward train, he's lost unless he's able to wake the owner up and ask him to take over. "Tell him to fuck off," the owner says. "There's a Shell station about twenty miles down the road."

"There's no way he'll make it that far, boss."

"Look, open the top drawer of the desk and take out the .38. It's always there. Take it out to him and tell him for me to shoot himself in the balls." He's right: the .38 is always there. Nobody knows better than Skinny Artemio why it's there and what it's to be used for. Sometimes he says to Riganti, "One of these days, I'm going to show up to find the boss has blown his head off."

"That's not the problem," Don Franco says. "The bad part is you'll be left without a job."

"Come on, Don Franco, don't talk that way."

"What way?"

"The rub is the poor guy has blown his head off."

"It's about time, Artemio. He should have done that a long time ago. If your only son dies, your wife takes her own life, there's nothing else left to do. You take your own life. Period. You know what your boss's problem is? He has no balls. He began to drink. Gained sixty pounds and spends the whole day sleeping. Did he buy the .38?"

"No, his wife did. She bought it and checked out. All in the same day."

"See what I mean? She had balls. Don't get all worked up,

Artemio. If the fat guy checks out on you, you come over here, where you'll have a job and a place to sleep safe and sound. Because there's not a chance in hell I'm going to check out. If I get the urge to kill someone, I'll kill you."

Artemio, frozen with fear, stands there staring at him without knowing what to say. If the fat guy kills himself, he thinks, it would be better to look for a job elsewhere. In Doña Juana's notions store, for example. Now he's just said, "It makes you mad. Mexico playing the World Cup and here we are watching from the outside!"

"Don't start up again with that," Parenti the barber tells him. "I'm not going to spend my life crying over that damned match with Peru."

Maybe this country has forgotten that great tragedy. Worse ones came later. Many worse ones. But in the middle of 1969, Argentina lost its chance to play in the 1970 World Cup in Mexico. Onganía, after the Córdoba uprising, needed a relevant sports triumph. He invited the all-star players to the Olivos presidential estate and subjected them to a barracks harangue: they had to win because there was nothing like soccer to make the people happy. The national all-stars were a disaster. Their only inspired player was the goalkeeper, Cejas. But a goalkeeper does not score goals. At best, he keeps them from happening. And he can't ever prevent them all. The decisive match was played in the Boca Stadium. It was against Peru, an outstanding team. Argentina had to win. But it doesn't win. It can barely scratch out a miserable tie, 2 to 2. The country sinks into melancholy.

"Artemio is right," Don Riganti says. "It's unpardonable that we didn't qualify. We're a country of cowards. We should have burned the Argentine Soccer Association down and hanged Pedernera and all the players, not by their balls, men, but by their necks, because we would have castrated them first."

"It was all a bunch of crap," Valentín, the guy who works for the state lottery, hisses. "Making Peru play in Boca Stadium. So we could shout them down. So the fans could browbeat them. Shit, they were sure afraid, right? If it weren't for Cejas and Marzolini they'd have made mincemeat of us."

"Fuck Marzolini! What did Marzolini do?" Anselmo, who has the newspaper and magazine stand, asks.

"He saved a goal, stupid!"

"Cejas also saved that goal."

Don Riganti bangs on the table. General silence. He says, "We should have killed the referee. Where'd he get off disqualifying Brindisi's goal? We were winning? If we'd made it 3 to 2, we'd have won!"

"I'm sorry, Don Franco," Skinny Artemio gets up the nerve to say. "But Brindisi knocked the ball out with his head."

"So what? If the referee had given him the goal, there'd have been no problem. What the hell difference would it have made to him to give the goal to Argentina in the Boca stadium? He didn't because he was an SOB."

"Or because the Peruvians bought him off."

"That's right, the Peruvians bought him off."

"It's a good thing Rendo made such a beautiful goal," Don Acébal says.

All of them, as if by magic, grow serene. They are overwhelmed by the sweetest and most healing of evocations.

"Rendo's goal was beautiful," Don Riganti says, thoughtfully.

"It came out of Cejas's cage," Artemio says.

"It sure did. Cejas handed it to him," Don Riganti says. "Rendo began to pace the field. He avoided all the Peruvians. All of them.Then he passed it off to Tarabini. Tarabini, that shit, out of sheer stupidity, sent it back to him. Rendo kept going. He dodged the goalkeeper and shot it in. What a player, by damn."

"No two ways about it," Valentín, the state lottery agent, said reflexively.

"Nope, no two ways about it," Artemio says, like an echo.

"We're the best," Don Riganti says. "There are no other players like ours. We won't be in Mexico. Because that's for sure, we're not. But it's just fucking bad luck we're not. Because you can't get way from it: we're the best. A round of wine for everyone, damn it!"

After a while Don Franco leans over confidentially to Acébal. Suddenly they seem isolated from the rest, alone.

"Tell me, Acébal, you know I'm your friend."

"Of course you are, Don . . ."

"Don't interrupt me. I know you're sad. Preoccupied. There's a real mess going on in the country. As you can see, nobody gives a damn. They prefer to talk about the World Cup. That's logical, because what the fuck do they have to do with this mess? If there were something they could do about it, maybe. But no, they've got to watch it from the sidelines. It's like the World Cup. It's being played far away and by someone else. But the World Cup is more fun. Your situation is different, Acébal. You've got them there, in your house. Well, it's not yours, but it's where you live. And there they are: the Catholic snot-noses and the thug of a General."

"I was just thinking, Don Franco."

"What?"

"What if those kids changed? What if they kidnapped Aramburu to kill him?"

"What are you trying to tell me?"

"That they're still Catholics. But that they've become Peronistas."

"How much wine did you drink, Acébal? Those snot-nosed Catholics, sons of oligarchs, of holier-than-thou oligarchs. Peronistas? Then what am I?"

"Another kind of Peronista."

"Acébal, if those kids are Peronistas, I'm Brigitte Bardot. Or something else."

"Something else, like what?"

"A first-class jerk."

"Don't run yourself down, Don Franco. Peronismo is something very complex. There's room for everything."

"Look, something good still might happen. Not that these kids turn out to be Peronistas. But that they turn out to be kidnappers. That they demand a gigantic ransom for Aramburu. They don't get it and they kill Aramburu. There, like that, you see? Like that, damn it. If they were to kill that son-of-a-whore thug, they're Peronistas. No matter what they think. Catholics or not. Killing Aramburu is to graduate as a Peronista. To go through your whole course of study with only one final exam. But the best one of all. The one that'll give you your degree forever."

"Don't talk nonsense, Franco. There's going to be real hell to pay. And in the end, just like always . . ."

"We'll be fucked over."

"You said it."

"Let's talk about something nicer. As I said, I know you've got something on your mind. I want to make it OK. You know I'm your friend. I want to make you happy. Look at that table over there, the one next to the window. Do you see it?"

"Yes, where María's sitting."

"Go over and sit down with her. She's waiting for you."

"Franco, María's twenty years old."

"What the fuck difference does that make to you? Let her handle it."

Don Acébal sits down in front of María. She's very pretty. She's a work of art, the kind of woman you call a *dusky Argentine*. As Acébal said, she's probably around twenty years old and her dark and taut skin glows because it's made of rock or the best wood, bearing the mystery of a complex race, which the white people, the ones in Buenos Aires, accept or reject, but which is impossible to ignore.

"How's it going, Don Acébal?"

"Happy to see you, kid."

"Look, Don Acébal, the boss asked me to make you happy. Today's gift. He's letting us use the nice second-story bedroom."

"Aha."

María closes the bedroom door. She turns the light on. Her back to Don Acébal, she takes her blouse and then her bra off. She turns toward him and looks at him with a smile. She knows very well that what she's showing is a work of art.

"My child, what gorgeous tits," Don Acébal says.

They're formidable but not large. Those tits, let us be honest, are in their greatest moment of splendor. You might say that's so because María is twenty years old. But the plenitude of a woman's tits has no age. It might not be until she's forty. They might not be at that moment a rock, an invincible turgidity, but maybe a warm languidness that falls into a man's hand so tenderly that it seems to have been made for it, resting there in such a way that the fortunate man feels they have been imagined for him by some god of love for that very moment, which is eternal or maybe outside of time. María's have the solidity of mountains. The freshness of rivers. Her nipples are perfect, dark and possessing a proud turgidness that makes them look heavenward. Don Acébal takes a step back from such beauty.

"Look, María, I'm up there in years. I'm not sure I'm going to be able to make you happy as you deserve."

"Dear Acébal, don't get it wrong. I'm the one who has to make you happy. You're here like a prince. Not to make someone happy, but to be made happy. I have two powerful motives. One, if I don't do it, Don Franco Riganti will beat the hell out of me. Second, I want to. You're a good man. You deserve it. I only ask one thing from you."

"Whatever you say, my child."

"If it doesn't all work like it should, if there are imperfections, if we only get halfway there—please don't tell Don Franco. I'll seek you out again, Don Acébal, and we'll go all the way, believe me. But today, when you leave here, when he asks you, tell the boss that it was the best fuck of your life. Promise?"

"Yes, my child, I promise. And I even have a presentiment. One the powerful erection I have this very moment tells me. Something I gave up for dead, María. What a revival."

"That makes me happy, Don Acébal. You won't have to lie to

the boss. I promise you, this is going to be the best fuck of your life. You'll never get another one like it."

He never does. Not even before the end of the year. That year, the one involving the crime at the La Celma Ranch, the World Cup in Mexico, Don Blas Acébal is found dead, dead and smelling bad among the weeds. He has been stabbed brutally enough to kill him and two others like him. The Buenos Aires Provincial Police cut off his hands (the same ones that caressed María's sublime tits) and take them to La Plata. They want, they say, to confirm his identity. No one knows anything about his family. They must have been too frightened to show their faces. Later the versions will flourish: that he saw a lot, that he said too much or that he refused to talk. Silly, vile things. The murmurings of the police, judges, newspaper reporters, of a swarm of insects that want to place poor Acébal in the middle of a complex story, full of detours in which a simple man like him ends up losing his way, his tame smallness dissipating like a morning fog. Too bad about that bloody ending. He must have suffered a lot. There is no such thing as a knife stab that doesn't bring shuddering pain to the body. At least we gave him a night of love.

The night of the thirty-first, Gaby Arrostito spent almost an hour looking at the typewriter. She has to type up the last communiqué. Fernando already wrote it and one supposes that she must obediently get it out. There's a problem. She doesn't like it. It's long. It's solemn. It's boastful. "Our organization has thus fulfilled the will of the people, which is ours also. If we have taken the life of this blood-stained general, it is because we are disposed to offer ours in the defense of our country so aggrieved by the enemies from without and the traitors from within. We would have preferred not to spill this blood. But so much has been spilled by those in power, by the enemies of the people, that all that was left to us was violence as the language to express ourselves. It is in the midst of this tragedy that the executioner Aramburu has died." *No, this won't do,* Gaby decides. The final communiqué must be a cross to the jaw, which is what Robert Arlt sought from literature. Short, dry, tragic, definitive. Fernando is going to become enraged. "Why didn't you send out the communiqué I wrote?"

"First, because it's no good. Second, because I write better than you do. You can't come to the point, Fernando. You have too many words to have killed a general. Say 'We killed him, we buried him,' put the date and sign it. That makes an impression.

That hurts. No words for the deceased. Only the bullets necessary to polish him off." She likes the idea: short, dry. There's a measure of disdain in that dryness. We don't give any explanations, sirs. We only inform. Understand that it's better to forget about Aramburu.

A large table made of rustic planks contains the dailies that she has been saving since last Friday, when it all began. *La Nación* from Saturday the thirtieth carries in large letters on the first page, "Former President Aramburu was kidnapped yesterday." Beneath it, "The government strongly condemns the act." *President / strongly.* What a shitty rhyme in Spanish. The newspapers of the regime use god-awful prose. They don't even know how to write. There's also a photograph of the crow Rojas. Short, with those sunglasses he wears to hide his macabre look, he is walking surrounded by other bastards wearing suits and ties, their hair short, with briefcases in which they carry documents no one should read, documents about illicit business dealings and million-dollar bribes. The legend under the photo reads, "The former provisional vice president, Admiral Isaac F. Rojas, as he arrives at the home of Lieutenant General Aramburu." What could the assassin dwarf have said? "Just imagine. This takes me by surprise. This expression of barbarism. Make no mistake: it's the work of Peronistas." Next to his is another photograph. Gaby becomes indignant. She has this guy marked. If it weren't for the fact he's a worthless asshole, she'd like to blow him away at the first chance. Next week. The guy calls himself a socialist. A socialist! With good reason the Peronista nation spits on anyone who talks to them about socialism. It's Américo Ghioldi. He's more furious than all the rest. His mouth is wide open. That's because he's shouting. That's the bastard who said, no sooner than they had shot Valle and his comrades, "The milk of clemency is gone." They call him "Norteamérico Ghioldi." A bullet up his ass would do him good. Or a good scare. Grab him one night when he's just getting home. When he's getting out of his car. Jab a gun in his gut right then and there. *Hey, Ghioldi, do you remember the milk of clemency? There's none left. It ran out again. Just yesterday, can you imagine. If it had lasted until today, you'd be saved. But no, old man, so we're going to have to shoot you three times in that bourgeois socialist gut of yours.* It's nice to see him beg, go down on his knees, plead for his children, for his wife, for the institutions, for the fatherland! *Stop begging, scumbag. We're not going to waste lead on you. We were just kidding. Go on home, shit your pants, get into bed, and let your wife serve you a bowl of hot soup.*

Gaby continues to look at the newspapers. *La Nación,* May 31: "No news about General Aramburu. Some arrests were made." *Were made? What sort of passive construction is that? How antiquated. They're reactionaries in everything. Even in their writing. Arrests! Who did they arrest? Jack the Ripper? That guy named Bustos who killed his wife, sliced her up in the bathtub, carefully packaged her up, and left bundles of her all over the city? That must have been fun. "Look, Mommy. There's a package here. Maybe it's a present someone dropped." No, son, it's a woman's head. Bad luck, lady. Now you're looking at twenty years of therapy for your son. The Government proposes to "frustrate the sinister designs" of the kidnappers. Sinister designs! Another crappy phrase.*

Suddenly, something serious: what Perón says from Madrid. Gaby doesn't like what she sees. And at that she doesn't trust Perón a whole lot. "The Old Man tells you something today and something else tomorrow," her comrades have said on more than one occasion. "He wants to be on everyone's good side. And you can't. You've got to choose." "Madrid, 30 (AFP)—The former president of Argentina, Juan Domingo Perón, who lives in exile in Madrid, denied any tie to the kidnapping of General Pedro Eugenio Aramburu in his declarations to France-Presse. He claimed that he had heard about the kidnapping from the Madrid morning newspapers. He expressed his concern for the acts of diverse groups that 'might lead Argentina,' he said, 'into a bloody civil war.'" The police that protect the estate of the former president, in the residential neighborhood of Puerta de Hierro, have been increased as of the night before. Perón is no fool. Anybody who thinks he is is stupid! The thug's astuteness. There's going to be a civil war, fellows. Either make a deal with me or the people will rise up in arms and shoot you down. *Crónica,* May 29: "Aramburu kidnapped." *Crónica,* May 30: "Aramburu—no leads." And a sensational photo: the doorman at the executioner's building sweeping the floor with a broom. He's not looking at the camera, merely taking care of the dirt. He's in a set of work clothes and you can tell that the whole business matters to him as much as shit. "Doorman: He failed to see a thing," the photo caption says. *Crónica,* May 31: "Independiente wins!" in huge letters, and below that, "River defeats Gimnasia; San Lorenzo ties." Reality has returned! Enough silliness. You've got to give the people what the people want. The readers of *Crónica* are grateful. They finally stopped boring the hell out of us with the stories about Aramburu. Down at the bottom, way down, in tiny letters: "The search for Aramburu continues. There are delays."

Gaby Arrostito is now sitting in front of the Lettera 32 again.

Come on, Gaby, get your courage up. You're right, come on. Gaby decides to ignore Fernando. The final communiqué will be brief. Dashiell Hammett style, damn it! Gaby has read everything he wrote. She begins:

MONTONEROS

COMMUNIQUÉ NO. 4

JUNE 1, 1970

TO THE PEOPLE OF THE NATION:

She smiles with satisfaction. Gaby is Gaby. No one is going to shove her around. She loves Fernando. She never loved anyone that way. He's her little hero. Her ballsy warrior. They'll be together up to the end. Win or lose. Life or death. Life is a risk; if not, it's nothing.

Now, yes. Now she sees it clearly.

She begins to type:

"The Montonero command . . ."

He comes out and looks at his comrades. There they are, seated around the large dining room table, biding their time, like hunters ready to get on with it and get back to town, leave the jungle. The jungle is always dangerous—strange territory where you plunge in with courage but almost always exit defeated. The time has come. Let us suppose that Firmenich says, "We can't continue to put this matter off."

Ramus picks up a bottle of beer and takes a long, hard swallow. Some foam comes out from the sides of his mouth, as though he were a mad dog. Something he's not. He's not mad. He only knows he doesn't want to stay here. He sets the bottle down noisily and exhales violently. It's not a burp but something like the sound of someone who's fed up, a vulgar and expressive noise that only means one thing: now, immediately, let's not waste any more time. Let's dispatch the executioner to fucking hell. The other comrade, "Julio," is not any gentler and doesn't show any more patience. He even utters the harshest and most direct words, the ones that could most upset Fernando: "It's only one shot, Fernando. One shot and we're out of here."

Ramus doesn't say a thing. Now, after a long reach, he's started to read one of the many newspapers from Buenos Aires. He's concerned his friend is letting him down. *Maybe he's taken*

pity on Aramburu. He talked to him too much. That was a mistake.
If you've got to kill someone, kill him. If you start talking with him,
he becomes something that's hard to kill, something that upsets you
and marks you: a guy, a human being. You've got to kill objectives,
not persons. Ideologies, not human beings. If the guy you've got to
kill, someone who's a tactical means, becomes an end in himself,
you've blown it. You make him strategic. You don't kill him. Come
on, you fool. Don't kill Aramburu; kill the person who shot Valle.
The person who organized the June 1955 bombing. The person who
made off with Evita's body. Damn it, Fernando, it's not up to me
to give you a list of what you already know by heart! We tried him
and we condemned him on the basis of that list of atrocities. Stop
digging into his soul, you jerk. What do you hope to achieve? To go
back in time? To discover in some way his humanity. If he has one,
it's not been much good to him. It never kept him from being the
first-class son of a bitch he always was.

Fernando, despite feeling all those pressures weighing down
on him, continues to exercise authority. He will do what he has
to do. What he needs to do. Whether the others like it or not.
To their surprise, he says, "I'll be right back. Wait for me. I won't
take long."

"What are you going to do?" Firmenich asks.

"Bad question, Pepe. Because there's only one answer: it's my
business." He walks away.

He walks the long corridor in solitude and goes into a small
room where he used to stay when he visited La Celma. In some
way it's *his* room. The one his friend and the Ramus family happily assign to him every time he shows up there. It's got the bare-
ness, austerity, and harsh minimalism of a cloister. He will search

there for that sacred entity of which he spoke so imprudently
with the Catholic general, who had the temerity—half in a swag-
gering way and half in his simple, powerful belief as a practicing
Catholic—to speak to him of the *fear of God*. The fear, as he is
stunned and troubled to discover, is with him. The only way to
confront it is to kneel down next to the bed and do something
that he hasn't done for a long time, something he always did as
a child, from the time he was a kid, but which he will do once
again, at that moment, before killing the General who is an assassin: pray.

He rejoins his comrades. Firmenich's not happy to see him.

"Did you talk to him again? Did it take you so long to say something so simple? 'General, we're going to rub you out.' That's all you had to say."

"He's not just anybody," Fernando says. He picks up a piece of bread and spreads butter on it. He doesn't know why, but talking to Aramburu made him hungry. What's the matter? Did something the condemned man said upset him? We don't know. We know the end is near and that it's Fernando who will have to kill him. Maybe he didn't need to know that beyond what was strictly necessary. Carlitos Ramus got it right: it's easier to kill a concept, an idea, than a guy. As far as Fernando was concerned, Aramburu was an ideological construct: the man who overthrew Perón, who had Valle shot, who hid Evita, the right-wing thug, the backup man for the regime. It made an impact on him when he tried to get free from his bonds. When he hurt his wrists. When he bled. That's when the General's fear became transparent. He had banned pity. He had read Clausewitz well: "Any consideration for the humane will weaken you," something like that. Is that why he spoke to Aramburu—out of a consideration for something humane? If that stupidity made his hand tremble at the decisive moment, he would not forgive himself.

"This country has yet to feel the full fury of the Argentine Army," Aramburu had said. *And what we've seen to date, what was it? A free sample? The previews for a horror film that hasn't opened yet? Cursed old man. It would have been better to tell him the decision and be done with it. Come on, General, we're going to kill you. And that was the end of it. Firmenich was right.*

Now he says, "I think you're making a mistake. Thinking he's a common type. One more thug. Important, but one more. Do us a favor: let's get this over with. If you go to talk to him again, I'll have to take him out myself."

"Take it easy, Pepe," Fernando says, and the vein in his forehead begins to throb again. Firmenich knows full well that he's dangerous when this happens. More than once he said, "If you ever see Fernando with the vein on his forehead swollen, get out of his way." Fernando says, "I'll execute the General. That's it. I'm the one in charge of the Command Operation. I'm the one who has to get his hands dirty." He picks up two guns lying on the table. One's a 9 mm. The other is a .45. He says, "Let's go."

By avoiding looking at him, the fury in Firmenich's face escapes him. That brought out a flashing like lightning in his eyes. He hears him say, "Hold on a minute, Fernando. There are a couple of things you're not seeing clearly. We're all getting our hands dirty in this together. If you think that putting the old man down makes you special, give me the gun and I'll rub him out myself. That's not what's important. You or me or Carlos. Any one of us. What we're doing is something else. We're the executing arm of the people's verdict."

"Why the trial, then?" Fernando asks.

"I already told Carlos. The trial was a sham. The real trial was not what we held today. The people have held it since 1955. Day after day. That trial took place in the conscience of the Peronistas. His death was decided there. And what is certain is that, by carrying it out, we get our hands dirty. We're going to sink them in shit and blood. We're sparing the people that. Why not if we're not their agent in arms? But we're *all* that agent. We're *all* getting our hands dirty. Not just you. No matter how much you're in charge. No matter how much, in the end, you're the one pulling the trigger."

Fernando looks at the other two. "You heard him?"

They nod.

"You're right," Fernando says. "Everything you've said is right." He thrusts the .45 down his back, supported by his belt. He takes the safety off the 9 mm. "OK, now let's go."

Lord, I ignored you for a long time. Too long. I don't know how long. I can't know. How can I know what's a lot or a little for Your eternal essence? As far back as I can remember, ever since I was a child or barely a young man who mumbled his prayers, I have sought to free You from me. Not to burden You with my actions. Not to be the judge of my errors, of what I did right. I always stuck to thanking You for the miracle of existence. Of the life You have given me. That was enough. The years went by and I discovered, painfully, the unjust world into which You let me fall. Even less did I reproach You or blame You for its contradictions, which are based wholly on the privileges of some and the needs of the rest. Man is free and responsible for the history he constructs. I've told You a thousand times: I don't want to be something You have to care for. It's enough for me to be Your creation. There will be others who will need You more than I do. I begged You not to turn Your gaze toward me. I'm free and that's enough.

Not this time, Lord. I'm about to take a life. I am going to kill. Many have killed before me. Men kill each other and seem uncon-cerned about Your Judgment and about Your commandment: Thou shalt not kill. How can I abide by it in a world in which no one abides by it? How could I not kill in a world whose law is death? A world in which the most powerful is the person who kills the most with the greatest impunity? I could do it without confessing it to You. Would You find out? I doubt it. Pardon me, but You do not seem to me to be very concerned about what happens to us. The evil triumph. Assassins go unpunished. Torturers walk the streets and no one points them out. Either out of fear or because they don't know what they have done. Do You know? If You do, you do not point them out, either. Nor do You punish them. My action is un-necessary. I could kill today, as I am getting ready to do, and not tell You. This is not a valley of tears. It is a valley of death. Of wars. Of tortures. Of injustices. A valley subjected to the rigor of the power-ful, to the indecent, profane, sinful ostentation of their wealth. To the unbridled industry of their arms, which never ceases. They kill the weak with these arms, Lord. And Evil has spread out offensively. In a way that humiliates us and, often, dispirits us. That way, Lord, since I believe only in Your sacred person and not in that fable about the Devil that frees You from the atrocities of this world by attribut-ing them to him, since I believe You to be all powerful and one, I believe that the essence of Evil necessarily exists in You, that You are no stranger to it. I surprise myself: I never thought it mattered to me. It does matter to me. The free sense of my free conscience is no longer, as it was in the past, enough for me. I find myself alone and I think that the act I am about to commit will assume incalculable dimensions. Should I do it? I'm not asking You. I know I will. But I need something from You for the first time. Because the fear I always had for You as a Catholic, the fear I lost for many years, the fear I banished from myself when I affirmed my liberty and I closed You out of my care, has come back to me. The General, who is an assas-

sin, is not the one who imposed it on me. That man surprised me. I suppose people who know they are going to die are either blocked by terror or attain unexpected levels of acuity, of penetration. The struggle for life brings both things. The desire to go on living has made that executioner dangerous. I took a risk: I exchanged too many words with him. My hand will not tremble at the precise moment. But he shook in me the fear that Catholics have toward You. Lord, I'll be brief: I'm going to kill him with a 9 mm pistol. I don't want to be alone when I do it. I beg You to look upon me. I'm not asking You to judge me or to let me know, somehow, that my action was just or that it wasn't. I know it will be just. I have thousands of reasons for knowing it. For killing him. I don't want to be alone when I do it. I want from You what I have never asked for: I want Your gaze. I need for You to see me. To be my witness. Since you know Good so well, as do you Evil, since the two are a part of Your nature that belongs to Eternity. I beg You to let me know, however You wish, by the sign that you choose, by even the slightest subtlety by which You draw near to me, if my action partakes of Good or of Evil. Do not believe that it will frighten me to know. Only that, to know. Not for You to judge me. Only to know. And knowing it, to face up to it. I have my truth; I want Yours. Do not hope for me to subject myself to it. I just want to know it. Why? To have a witness. Whether my action partakes of Evil or partakes of Good, I could not accept any condemnation on Your part. If I exercise Evil You cannot condemn me, because You also exercise it. I demand Your valuable opinion by being my witness, by watching me. Perhaps I will respect it more than I am now disposed to admit. Maybe even it will hurt me. But I doubt it. As I judge things, Good and Evil, the two pos-

sibilities, lie with You. Neither will negate You, and neither will lead me away from You. There are too many horrors in the world and, if You exist, it is not possible to accept that You are wholly good, that Evil is not part of Your essence, immortal like You. Lord, I want You to watch me. I want Your eyes on me. This I ask of You and I swear that I will never ask another thing of You. Amen.

Aramburu watches them come in. There they are: they've come to kill him. No more time for words. Each one knows where the other one stands. What he's thinking. What he wants to do. Especially, in his case, what he did. Is Aramburu thinking about Valle? Not likely. *They're not going to kill me for what happened to Valle. I'm a symbol. The guy who threw Perón out. One knows the risks he takes.* He should have foreseen this. But he never imagined that kids like this could show up. Revolutionaries and Peronistas, vengeful, irresponsible or courageous, it's all the same thing. But with balls. Hell, who'd have thought it?

They take the bonds from his hands. Aramburu rubs his wrists. They're swollen and there's some blood.

"We're very sorry about this, General," Fernando says. "If it were up to me, we'd have avoided this."

"It's within the rules," Aramburu concedes. "You always tie prisoners up. A prisoner who escapes ceases to be one. A kidnapper without a prisoner, too."

"There's more to us than just kidnappers," Firmenich insists.

"How's that?"

"We are your judges. We tried you and found you guilty."

"And now you're going to execute me."

"Exactly."

"May I make a request, judge?"

"Are you being ironic?"

"Was there any irony in my voice?"

"I don't think so."

"Because there wasn't."

"What would you like to request from me, General?"

"Something silly. But I would not like to go to my death with the chance of doing something clumsy that would make me look ridiculous. You understand me, don't you?"

"Completely, General. What would you like?"

"Tie my shoes."

"Sorry. I hadn't noticed."

Firmenich goes down on one knee and ties Aramburu's shoes. He stands up. He looks at him. Aramburu says nothing.

"We have to tie your hands behind your back," Fernando says.

"Tie my hands again? Just look at my wrists. They're a mess."

"Not really, General," Fernando says. "They're in tune with the circumstances. That's the way things are. When one goes before a firing squad, it's always with the hands tied behind the back."

"Is a firing squad awaiting me?"

"Don't ask questions when you know the answers."

"Not completely. I know there's no firing squad. How are you going to kill me, then?"

"You'll know soon enough." Fernando looks at his comrades. With his usual brevity, harshly, with that steely tone he knows how to use to give orders, he says, "To the basement."

"Just a minute," Aramburu protests. "Like this? I can't even shave?"

"Why do you want to shave?" Ramus says tensely. "No one's

going to see you."

"I'm going to see me. I never thought I'd die dirty. You've got to at least allow me to take a bath."

"General," Fernando says in a loud and somewhat irritated voice, "stop messing around. God will take you in His arms no matter how you reach Him."

"I always thought I'd be clean."

"Our Lord is only interested in the cleanliness of the soul. Think about whether this is what you have to offer him. If you think you already thought about it, think about it again. Just in case."

"Not even Saint Augustine had that to offer."

"Saint Augustine was a tormented sinner. Only his great suffering washed away his sins. I see no great suffering in you."

"I don't see it in you, either, and you are about to commit a supreme sin."

"Maybe. But if we repent, it won't be today. We have time."

Fernando becomes very serious. His eyebrow furrows and two vertical and deep gashes appear between his eyebrows. "We promised something to you. We are going to pray for the salvation of your soul. Today, General."

"I want a priest," Aramburu demands.

"We can't do that," Firmenich says. "Don't play with us. You're trying to trick us to the very end. What makes you think we could bring a priest here? All the roads are under surveillance. They'd follow him. They'd find us. It would have been all for naught."

"What do you mean?" Aramburu says incredulously. "You don't have a priest? Did you think to bring one? Or have him here, awaiting us? What kind of Catholics are you? I wouldn't have refused you a priest. If I'd had to shoot you, the first thing I'd have done would have been to line one up. Valle had one, in case you didn't know. He had his parish priest, Monsignor Devoto. He could give him an embrace. Discharge his sins, receive absolution. Where's mine? Valle's daughter was with him until the end. She reviewed the firing squad, which respected her. One of the soldiers broke and was crying. He told her, 'I swear I won't fire.' Who's going to say that to me?"

"No one," Fernando blurts out. "Stop blackmailing us. What priest was with the men massacred in José León Suárez? What priest fed the persecuted Peronista workers, left hungry by your dictatorship? What priest was with Felipe Vallese? What priest was there for each one of the populist militants who died for Perón during the last fifteen years?" He calms down. He does not want to destroy the solemnity of the execution. He does not want, right now, in the culminating moment, for everything to collapse. He says, calmly, "Enough, General. Walk over there toward the basement."

"And my family?" Aramburu says. "What'll happen to them?"

"We'll send them your effects. And nothing more, General. Your family is not at risk. The regime will take care of them like royalty. Like suffering victims. Like those who will spend the rest of their lives weeping for the hangman of Perón's Argentina. Come on, get walking."

They reach the basement stairs. It's old and unsafe. The handrail is wobbly. There's not much light. The basement is as old as the house. It's at least seventy years old. It's a narrow and lugubrious place. In February 1969, looking for weapons, the founding group of the Montoneros attacked the Federal Firing Range in

Córdoba. A simple operation, but one that yielded more than they'd anticipated: a mountain of rifles they ended up storing in this basement. Now the stairway shakes dangerously. And if you take into account the fact that Aramburu's hands are tied, the situation becomes wrenching. Firmenich precedes the General, protecting him, keeping him from falling.

They reach the basement. The place is tiny, primitive, and barely measures a few feet long.

Then Aramburu asks, "You're going to kill me here? In this basement?"

Fernando is a young man with firm convictions and rapid responses. "Here, General. Right here. I suppose you must feel it unworthy of you. You'll have to deal with it."

"And you reproach me for executing Valle in the National Penitentiary? You guys are going to shoot me in a basement?"

It's a violent dialogue, with no going back. The stridency of the voices, the tones, nothing matters. The violence lies in what they say. These are the last words they exchange and they possess the dramatic quality of final, extreme questions, ones in which life, death, and honor are discussed.

"There are things you cannot understand, Aramburu," Fernando says, freeing his prisoner at last of the weight on him. "You shot Valle and you were the president of the republic. The most powerful man in the country. You could have killed him in Government House if you'd wanted to. You had every means. Since you did, only cruelty, only hatred explain the fact that you sent him before the firing squad of a penitentiary."

"And what is the meaning of the fact that you kill me in this basement?"

"I'm not killing you," Fernando says, as curt and firm as always. "I'm sentencing you. I stand for the will of the people. We are the justice of the people."

"Don't screw with me! You're a high-handed shit of a brat. The people don't even know what you're doing. Nor will they find out. I don't know if those people you invoke so much, the Peronista nation, would want you to kill a general of the republic in a basement. They're working, pacifist people. You don't even know them."

"I'm not going to discuss that."

"You're afraid to discuss it. There are many fighting Peronista militants. But the majority, the bulk of them, are not combative. They're not violent. They don't want to kill. They want the return of the happy days of the Peronista nation. They're workers. They're lower-middle class: employees, skilled laborers, notaries, bookkeepers, lawyers without powerful clients, teachers of all levels. They love Perón. They followed him and they'll continue to vote for him. We can't de-Peronize them. We cannot make them into followers of our democracy. That's how we got into this mess. Military government, civilian government, again a military one, again a civilian one. Enough! The people are not waiting for Perón to show up disguised as Castro, as Mao, or as the leader of the Third World. The Perón they're waiting for is the Perón they knew. You think history changed. The Peronista nation doesn't want changes. They want the historic Perón. The Perón of the welfare state, generous and openhanded. They want the return of the fatherland of happiness, not war. Listen to me, God damn it! The simple workers and employees and honest skilled laborers don't want power—much less the war and blood to win it!

They want Perón. Feeling themselves once again protected by his generous hand. Celebrating the First of May. Listening to Hugo del Carril singing, 'This is the fiesta of work. United by the love of God.' They want peace, work, and vacations. You're the ones who want war."

"The Peronista nation has changed. Who made the Córdoba rebellion? The one in Rosario? The one in Mendoza? They did."

"That's a lie. The combative SITRAC-SITRAM unions did. The left-wing leaders like Tosco. Did you ever hear José Ignacio Rucci talk about Tosco? That Trostkyite pinko, he calls him. That Marxist. Even that guerrilla spits in his face."

"You don't understand a thing, Aramburu," Firmenich says. "You're misinformed. That tame Peronista nation died. You guys killed it. By persecuting it, jailing it, torturing it, banning its rights. Denying its leader. The years don't pass in vain, General. That people, today, in this Argentina degraded by years of mockery and illegal dictatorships, *is* different. It will receive the news of your death with glee. There will be fiestas in the shanty towns. Cheap wine, sweet and thick. Or sweet and claret but fatal for making one lose one's head. They're going to dance. To have hope. Let me repeat, General: *hope.* Because your death will give hope to the downtrodden of Argentina. That is, to whom? The Peronistas, by damn! Don't expect a tame and cowardly people to refuse to greet us for having done away with the greatest of the thugs. We will be heroes. We know what we're doing. We took on a collective aspiration and we're carrying through on it. That's enough. That will make us demigods, General. Did you hear that? demigods?"

"Then let's talk about something else," Aramburu says, gripped with fury. "How large is this basement? Six, eight feet? Tell me, where are you going to place your firing squad?"

Firmenich gets ready to answer, but Fernando stops him short with a brief wave of his hand. "Take it easy," he says. "This is up to me. You've spoken too much, Pepe." He stares at Aramburu. He says, "There's not going to be any firing squad. Get this straight, General: we are a revolutionary organization. You were the state. You could have the luxury of firing squads. We can't. We work in clandestinity. Do you know what clandestinity is? It means living in basements. You're dying at the hands of clandestine men and your death is a clandestine death. We can offer you only this basement."

Aramburu sits down on a bench against the wall. Now he looks tired. But he rebounds.

"You aren't going to be able to kill me with rifles. With rifles. An execution is an execution because of the weapons used. Rifles. It's always been that way."

"The execution will be by pistol," Fernando says. "There's no room for anything else."

"Who's going to do it?"

"I will. The head of the operation."

"OK, but try to understand this: you are not shooting me. You're giving me the coup de grâce. It's the coup de grâce you administer from the distance in which you are getting ready to shoot me. The coup de grâce is different from a shooting. The squad that does the shooting doesn't know who's killed the condemned man. Then someone proceeds to the coup de grâce—a very impressive act because the one who administers it knows he's the one who gives it to the poor man left still alive. It's at close range. If you will allow me, that looks a lot like a close-range assassination. That's what you're about to do. You're going to assassinate me."

"You fucking old man!" Firmenich shouts. "You're trying to trick us with scumbag military dialectics. Where did you learn that? In the School of the Americas?"

"No," Aramburu says. "I've just learned it. You're going to assassinate me."

Fernando smiles through his clenched teeth. "You were tried by a revolutionary tribunal. You are an assassin. A defender of the regime of exploitation that oppressed our country. A man who insulted Eva Perón, a woman who was more worthy than you or all of us are. I don't care where or when I execute you. I know I have to do it. And that this act is just. And that I, by doing, am just also." He turns to his men. "Come on. You, Pepe, start tapping out Morse code with a key. We've got to stifle the sound of the shots."

"Why? No one can hear a thing."

"Do what I say."

"You're the one who doesn't want to hear the shots, jerk," Aramburu says. "But you will. And they will explode in your head for the rest of your life."

"Leave," Fernando tells his men.

They leave.

Fernando and Aramburu are left alone.

Fernando takes out the 9 mm.

"You won't suffer, General," he says.

"I don't care if I suffer. I regret losing my life."

"We're done with words." He raises the pistol and points at Aramburu's body. At most, there's barely a yard between them. Aramburu stands up. Not only that—he stretches himself to offer his chest. Fernando is not surprised. He would have been surprised by something extreme, final, on the part of his victim. Something operatic. Like breaking down, beginning to cry, begging for mercy, talking about his family, or mentioning a grandson—someone who would be left devastated by his death, left all alone. No, nothing of the sort. The man standing in front of him looks at him in sadness, but fearlessly. Nor does his steeliness seem to come from his condition as a Catholic, as if he believed that a bountiful God awaited him some place in the universe to grant him consolation, to take him unto Him. If something keeps him from despair it is not in the Gospels. It is within him. Perhaps men need not have been good nor have been just to die with serenity. It's enough for them just to have believed that they were. It's also enough that they don't care. There are men who pass through life without ever judging themselves morally.

They exhaust themselves in action. There is so much to be done that it is ridiculous to ask themselves if what they are doing is good or bad. They are the ones who have the best death. Death is only another fact of life. Its only difference is that it's the end for everyone. Because it is the last one. Where, then, does Aramburu's serenity come from? It's difficult to know. But let us risk an answer: from his failure. Failure makes men serene—gives them a sense of relief. There are no more risks; without illusions there are no deceptions; without future there are no anxieties; without plans there are no enemies. Only sadness remains, the acceptance of a fateful, unresolved destiny and nothing more. Thus Aramburu looks at Fernando in the way we have said: with sadness but without fear. And if he were to become infuriated? Or isn't it undignified to die precisely when one has plans, so many things to do yet in this world? Here we propose another point of view, not far removed from the previous one, but one that enriches them: Aramburu has just understood that his plan was impossible. That he was impossible. That he had awakened many hatreds, that he was responsible for many deaths, that he was guilty as far as many consciences were concerned, the passionate judgment of too many men, guilty, directly or indirectly, for everything—because the other, Rojas, had earned for himself the characterization as clumsy, as an animal. He, to his misfortune, was intelligent, the clever thug, the wisest of all, the one who stood for all the losses, all the death, because he was the leader, the one who did the best thinking. The one who was absolutely guilty. How could he now pretend to be the guarantor of national unity? If one leaves a wake of hatred, at some point his terrible past returns to settle accounts. This is what has happened here, in Timote. This somewhat hallucinatory young man who is about to kill him is the confluence of fifteen years of mistakes. If it's History that's going to shoot you, why cry, why break down? Whom are you going to beg for clemency? History bypasses, leaves behind those it has condemned, and proceeds on its way.

"I am going to proceed, General."

Aramburu maintains his position. They look at each other for the last time. Aramburu says, "Proceed."

Fernando fires. He shoots him in the chest. Not in the heart. Not in the head. In the chest. That's where the bullet enters.

Aramburu reels backward and ends up in the opening between the bench and the wall. But his blood splatters the walls. And it even stains Fernando's shirt. And his face.

Fernando goes over to him. And he delivers more shots with the 9 mm. Then he puts the 9 mm away and takes out the .45. He shoots him again. In the head. Again the blood splatters him. Perhaps he thinks the old man had too much blood. He didn't expect it.

He takes him out of the corner where he is and lays him on the floor. He discreetly covers him with a blanket. That blanket is not there by chance. It's there for two reasons. Fernando believes that the dead deserve respect. That they are defenseless against the gaze of the living. That there is always an undefinable sensation of superiority in the person who views a body. He does not want this dishonor for Aramburu. And also, the body of Aramburu is not an easy one to view—especially if you're the one who killed him. It prefigures so many things: revenge, catastrophe, scandals, persecution. And blood. He wasn't expecting that fact. Just like the way one of the many things Aramburu says rings, whispers, and even at times howls in his conscience, obsessively, like a ceaseless kettledrum, maintaining a systematic rhythm, measured and lugubrious, but now made by that blood foreboding, terrifyingly prophetic: "My blood will call for yours."

He goes over to the stairs.

"Come down here, damn it!" he shouts.

The others appear. Stealthily, they enter one by one. They see the body on the floor, with that blanket, protected, respected. They imagined Fernando would do that. Keep them from seeing the body. For himself, because he had killed him. For Aramburu, because a dead man is always defenseless. Because even though it's the body of a man, it's not that man. It's what remains of him. A carcass. A thing. They are surprised by the vision of the abusive blood, which climbs the walls, which forms, at its two extremes, claws or feet of savage birds. Did the old man have that much blood? Doesn't the weight of years make men dry up as they get older? Isn't that why their passions fade? Where did they get such an idea? Only because they were so young. They surely had seen old guys turn red to the point of bursting. When they swear. When they lose their patience. Or lose control when least expected. When they hate. When they shout, when they threaten. No, the world's full of ruddy old men.

"He was a vampire," Fernando says, seeing them paralyzed by the blood the moment they walked in. "That's Valle's blood. The blood of the June bombing. The blood of those massacred in José León Suárez. The blood of Tanco. Of Cogorno. The blood of all those he had killed. Even Felipe Vallese's. It's all the blood spilled by the Argentine thug. Look where it all was. In the body of the one most guilty. He had fed himself on it. Like Dracula."

It's 7:30 in the morning, June 1, 1970. They all know what to do. They begin to dig a grave. They dig deep, as if urged on by that old fear of the dead coming back. That's why we bury them, so they'll rest in peace and so we'll be at peace. They finish their task.

"Come over here," says Fernando, who is standing next to the body. He says, "I'm going to pull the blanket back. I want us all to see the dead body. Carry that image in our hearts. The dead body of that General who was an assassin is our work. Our first big operation. It required his life and it is going to require the lives of others. We are at war. Maybe it will be fierce and long enough to require our own lives."

He pulls back the blanket and they all look at Aramburu's body. Fernando covers it again. They place it in the grave. They throw three bags of lime on it. Fernando, not in a low voice but to himself, for his veiled interiority, in some fold or recess of his conscience, mediates, saying, "What a disgrace, General. Look at how they will find you. It will be difficult for them to recognize you when they take you out of here. Is this Aramburu, the great man? And you'll be wearing a shirt and pants, unshaven. Stinking, General. Don't forget that detail. You, who must have been the sort to use expensive scents, is going to cast on the others the smell of the grave, of rot, of industrious worms. You will not have your uniform on. Nor your medals. Nor your decorations from foreign governments. Especially, the uniform. A general without a uniform is not a general. He's not even a soldier. He can't even give an order. Not only because he's dead, but because he's almost naked. And now, if Valle's wife were to come to see you, please don't fail to tell her that. Tell her *the president is sleeping.*

Because now you are, General. Now you'll sleep for all eternity, without end. Don't think we don't have any pity for you, don't think we don't say prayers for your immortal soul. We're Christians. We're not Marxists, we're not atheists. We believe there's a God and that He is going to take pity on you. But we're fighting Christians. We have come to help those the prophet of Nazareth described in his sermons. The poor in spirit. The poorest of the poor. And the death of others does not frighten us. Why should it frighten us if our own death frightens us even less? Why would we hesitate to take their lives if we have decided to offer our own in this struggle? Why would we hesitate, were the time to come, in sacrificing innocent lives if we are ready to sacrifice our own, which are also innocent? Not many will understand this, General. But if we, who are innocent, give up our lives for a cause that is larger than we are, which is more than our miserable individual existences, what is going to keep us from taking the lives of others, who are also innocent, but guilty, General? Guilty for not risking themselves in the liberation of the fatherland, guilty for being comfortable, for seeking the rotting triumph of bourgeois life, guilty for being cowards, for being indifferent to injustice, to the suffering of the majority? The Gospel, of whose truth we are warriors, speaks very clearly the message of Jesus. He not only came to bring love. He also brought the sword. One must love and one must hate. And if loving the poor demands hating and even taking up the sword against those who exploit them, that is the path that charts our faith. God is love. But, in us, love is fighting against injustice. Love is war and we are ready to carry our earthly battle where our faith takes us. And that faith, General, is boundless. It is not the Sunday faith of the bourgeois, capitalist family. It is not the simple faith of the coalman, never subjected to the proof of doubt. It is not the faith of the capitalists of the Church, who have forgotten the people, who have placed God in the service of the powerful. It is the faith of those who do not hesitate to pursue any extreme in their struggle on behalf of the poor. It is the faith of a whirlwind: it carries us beyond ourselves. It makes us better. It finds in our hearts passions we were not aware of. By putting us in the service of the humiliated, it puts us in the service of the Gospel of Jesus. It allows us to understand the one profound meaning of the word of the prophet of Nazareth. The Kingdom of Heaven is not for the rich. If it were, a camel would pass through the eye of a needle. The rich will never inhabit the Kingdom of the Lord because of their greed, their lack of love for the poor, for the hatred they direct toward them, in the suffering burden to which they subject them, for the greed with which they pay them, for the violence with which they punish any form of rebellion, for their sloth, for their lasciviousness, for believing more in the obscene materiality of their wealth than in the wealth of divine spirituality, which is unique."

As if it were possible, Fernando draws even more within himself. He rests his chin on his chest. His companions hear him say—in a clear and reasonable voice and with the deliberation, the Christian sentiment of pity which he cannot hide—"May God, Our Lord, have pity on your soul. Amen."

"Amen," they all say.

They wait until night to return to Buenos Aires.

They speak little during the day. Fernando spends his time sleeping.

At around 8:00 PM they leave Timote.

They travel in the Gladiator pickup. It's completely dark. There is a high moon, as perfectly round as something drawn by an infallible, perfect compass. Stars are out. It's a splendid autumn night. Fernando takes over the driving. Firmenich doesn't like it. He sees him assuming everything. If he doesn't do it, it's done poorly or not at all or it gets botched. It's the vice, the high-handedness, and even the dementia of bad leaders that makes them feel themselves irreplaceable. Never to delegate anything. In the end they gambled their lives in all of the operations and they're screwed in the dumbest one of all. Fernando will need watching. No one kills Aramburu and remains the same person. It's possible that Pepe is not wrong. Maybe Fernando feels himself the incarnation of History. The avenger of all the martyrs of Peronismo. That would be a pity. It would be to give Firmenich an advantage, making it easier for him to go the route he aspires to, the one that will make him the leader of the organization. Because Pepe is a guy with ambitions. Too many. He's no Fernando. Fernando is in your face. There're no two ways with him. If he hates you, he hates you. If he loves you, he loves you. If he kills you, he kills you, as we well know. Pepe is roundabout, rustic. Fernando's loss would leave the leadership in his hands—something that, we insist, would not displease him. What's more, it's what he wants. We know what we're saying. But often, perhaps clumsily, like inexperienced narrators, we end up saying things twice. Not just to say them. Rather to brand them with fire. We prefer the anger of the reader over a couple of repetitions to the risk of overlooking some essential topics. If heights make Fernando dizzy, if he loses his head over the momentous nature of his action, if he believes in it (Firmenich enjoys an instant of the precision of this unfathomable and, yet, popular concept that is so much ours: *to believe in it*), if he plays the part of the macho with Gaby, to whom he now delivers up the most spectacular body the organization will have in its history, no matter even if he kills half of Argentina, no matter how much he kills Onganía, Lanusse, Rojas, he will always have to be prepared for a situation peculiar to revolutionary groups that undertake spectacular acts: dementia, the delusions of grandeur of its protagonists—even more so if there is one protagonist, a single one, with all of the glory for him, and even more so if he is the type with the sang-froid and the talent to claim that glory for himself, to make it his own even if it isn't his wholly, to make it his own because he gave the final blow, because he was leading the operation. Fernando has too much talent and too much advantage, a methodical, precise intelligence like a Swiss watch, patiently or recklessly ardent but always seeking the exact balance, the exact point to strike the blow; now he has it all, now he has it all, he's got to be patient—he even has Gaby, who must be waiting for him proud and ardent, a cat in heat, driven mad to have a tumble with the macho whose hand did not waver, the crazy dude who punctured History, who avenged all the vanquished, all the torturers, all the miserable of the earth, the most macho one of all, the leader, the best hung one of all, the horniest, the one who'll fuck her tonight and tell her, and she'll come listening to him say it, "You're being fucked by the guy who blew Aramburu away. Skinny, History is fucking you." *Stupid shit. Go ahead, fuck her. She's yours. It's all yours. I'd have to kill Perón to beat you out. But that would be like killing God. Or worse, like committing suicide. I'm not going to commit suicide. No one, ever, is going to get that from me. I'll bide my time. That's all. Wait for you, Fernando. I know how to wait. They've all been mistaken. Everybody screws up sometime, blows it, fucks up. Especially heroes. The great individualists. Look at Che. No one has anything to say about Che. It's all respect and veneration. Saint Ignatius of La Higuera! Give me a break. There wasn't a way in which the heroic guerrilla didn't screw up. Why? Because he was Che. Because he believed in it. Castro is another story. Castro will last. He knows the revolution is not an adventure. That you don't run around from one place to the next offering yourself. Revolution is patience. And if he has to follow gray roads, uncertain paths, without any kind of heroics, then fuck it. But it's what you've got to do. Fernando doesn't know this. He's not made that way. He's like Che. A firecracker tossed up in the sky, illuminating everything but burning itself out. I'll wait for you, Fernando. Patience is what I've got a lot of. I know: sooner or later, and I think sooner, you're going to drop the leadership like ripe fruit into my hands.*

He observes him. Fernando has his eyes fixed on the road. It's a shitty road. A dirt road, with potholes, damp. You skid and you'll end up head first in a ditch. What's more, Fernando is not afraid to speed.

"What are you thinking?" he asks him.

Fernando doesn't answer. He doesn't hear Firmenich's question. *With Aramburu dead, the Montoneros acquire a mythic prestige among the Peronistas. It wasn't an assassination. We did what the people wanted. We did justice. The justice of the people. We passed sentence on the bloody thug. It was in the spirit of the times. It's in the heart of the poor. The ones who have a photo of Evita in their homes and one of Perón on a dappled horse. The ones who still place candles before the photo of Evita. Because for them she is a saint. The saint refuted by Aramburu and the likes of him. Now they are going to let up. Either they give us Evita or we will continue to blow them away. If they give us Evita, we won't give her to Perón. We'll go to the shantytowns, No. 31 especially, and we'll put her in the hands of the poor, those she helped. She's one of them and she belongs to them. She lived for them and they must have her. And then we'll create an open organization. The young people are going to fall in love with us. The youth want guerrillas, guys who'll gamble their balls. They clamor for vanguards. We'll give them the best of all. To hell with the election plans of the military. "Neither votes nor boots but guns and balls"—how grand that sounds. And then we'll drag the Old Man into it. And we'll say to him, "General, you are the leader, but we are the revolutionary vanguard organization and, without us, you'd never have returned. Of course, then, you'll be in charge of strategic leadership, as always. But that leadership you will now share with us. That's what's necessary, General. Because of your age. Because you've got to think hard about who's going to succeed you. And who if not us? The ones who brought* you back. The ones like us who gambled our balls, risked our lives, liquidated thugs wholesale. "Leadership, leadership / Montoneros and Perón." And if you don't like it, learn to, see. Because there are so many things we're going to do. We are going to accumulate so much power in this country that either you join us or you go back to Madrid, with your bandit puppies, your slippers, with that whore Isabelita, third-rate cabaret dancer, the comical bad copy of Eva. The only one. Who if she were still alive, would be with us. In this pickup, General. Getting the hell out of Timote. Happier than ever, because at the most critical moment, when I was descending the stairs to off Aramburu, she told me, "Hold on, kid. Don't deprive me of that pleasure." And she offed him. I don't mean she pulled the trigger. I'm not crazy, General. I'm not crazy and I don't believe spiritist fairytales. But I'll swear something to you, I swear it on my honor: when I shot the thug who was a killer, she was the one who was in my heart, giving me courage. She was the one who told me, "Blow him away, kid. Have no mercy. Kill him in the name of all those he killed. Kill him for me. Because it's because of him I'm not among you. The people can't offer me flowers. Kneel before my tomb. Pray. Cry. Beg. In the chest, kid. No holding back. Don't think of God. He's got nothing to do with this. God does not see you. God is not in this basement. It's just us, we Peronistas. And our thirst for vengeance."

"Pardon me, ma'am," I dared to say to her. "I want God to be in this basement. And I believe he is. I want him to see how much I'm putting at risk the salvation of my immortal soul for the love of my people. Many will say I'm an assassin. Others, an angel of revenge. For the justice of the people, who chose to become incarnate in me. What can I say? To whom will I turn when I am in doubt? To

*Him, ma'am. That's why He's got to be here. So He'll know. So He
will hold as a bounty the truth and deliver it to me in my moments
of doubt."* The voice of Eva came to me like a hurricane, with the
urgency of someone who no longer has any time to lose. *"Enough of
talking, kid. Pull that trigger and let's be done with this matter right
now. If you need God to be in this basement so much, screw you.
Because He's not. Where the hell do you want Him to be? This act
is yours, Fernando. God does not kill for you. You're the one killing Aramburu. If by doing so you're an assassin or an emissary of
the justice of the people, you'll have to carry that problem on your
shoulders. You're going to have to settle it. And maybe you never
will. So what, kid? Not everything's yes. Not everything's a no. But
let me tell you something. It's very simple. It has the monumental
simplicity of the great truths: he who kills to avenge the humilia-
tions that the powerful have inflicted on the people does not kill. He
does justice. So fire, damn it! Enough of doubts, enough of words,
enough of absent or present gods. I want the truth of the executioner, Fernando. I want to see him bleed to death."* I pulled the trigger.
And Eva's voice died away, vanished, with the explosion of the bullets. I was left alone. The body of the executioner and me. And that
damn blood all over the place. Damn it, too much blood.

*Look what a beautiful night it is, General. The stars barely fit
in the cloudless sky. And the moon is round, immense. As though
it wanted to illuminate our triumph today and even those to come.
And she's waiting for me. Gaby, General. She may not have Evita's
balls, but she's not far from it. Boy, they'd have sure gotten along.
What a political team Eva would have had with Gaby at her side!
But she's mine, General. I need Gaby. She's a great gal. She's seven
years older than I. She's read* Das Kapital. *She explained it to me*

from cover to cover, General. Between one fuck and another, if
you'll pardon me. A great gal, as I was saying. Seven years older than
I. Sometimes I feel like a boy alongside her. But not today. Today
Gaby will have a giant in her arms. And I will feel young and strong
and crazed, sweating and hard as a stake when I penetrate her and
make her mine, just as the years to come belong to me.

Then, as if by accident, he unexpectedly lets out a sentence
that everyone hears, because it jumps out of his mouth, rich, full
of hope, flush with the future.

Let us suppose he says, "No one can stop us."

He steps on the gas.

MONTONEROS

COMMUNIQUÉ NO. 4

JUNE 1, 1970

TO THE PEOPLE OF THE NATION:

The leadership of the Montoneros communicates that today at 7:00 AM
Pedro Eugenio Aramburu was executed.
May God, Our Lord, have mercy on his soul.

PERÓN OR DEATH — LONG LIVE THE FATHERLAND

WITHDRAWN

No longer the property of the
Boston Public Library.
Sale of this material benefited the Library.

About the Author

Philosopher, novelist, essayist, and screenwriter **José Pablo Feinmann** has helped make philosophy a celebrated topic in the newspapers and on the airwaves of Argentina, where he studied and taught philosophy at the university of Buenos Aires.

WITHDRAWN
No longer the property of the
Boston Public Library.
Sale of this material benefited the Library.